TWO
DARK
MOONS

TWO DARK MOONS

AVI SILVER

MOLEWHALE PRESS

Published by Molewhale Press
www.molewhalepress.com

First Edition

Print edition ISBN: 978-1-7752427-2-7

Cover art and interior illustrations by Haley Rose Szereszewski
haleyroseportfolio.com

Map and book design by Sienna Tristen

The author gratefully acknowledges the creators of the following type-faces, which were used in designing the text of the book: 'Gentium Basic', 'Garamond Pro', 'Sqwoze', 'Century Gothic'

To everyone who has ever been told
they are too much.

Prologue

IT WAS THOUGHT TO BE BAD LUCK to give birth beneath a moonless sky, but Lahni Par was very quickly learning that this baby did not care.

The pain had come nearly three lunar phases early—a rush of water and a low clenching in her belly as she was packing to make the biennial crossing with the rest of the hmun, her village. One look at her face and her husband went pale, rushing off to find his mother and his composure. Any other day she would have teased him for knocking over their bags on his way out the door; under any other lunar phase she would have laughed at her misfortune, charmed by the child's hereditary impulsiveness. *A good trader*, she might have said. *So eager to come and explore!*

It was harder to plan for the future of one that might be exiled from the mountain not an hour out of the womb.

Outside, all was stars, freckles on the face of a sightless god. The unsteady twinkling was beautiful but offered no

1

divine truth for the people to interpret. This was the Minhal lunar phase, a time of unguided darkness as the moons Ama and Chehang averted their eyes from the mortal world below. A bad time for babies—any child ignored by the gods in birth had no chance of thriving into adulthood.

And though it was unfortunate, the wisdom passed down by the oracles of Ateng was as clear as it was bruising: *Cast out this unfortunate soul, for it brings only disorder to the hmun.*

So Lahni laboured quietly. She bit down on a rag, and she dug her nails into her husband's arm, and she followed along with his whispered prayers in her head. Her back felt fit to split like a nightflower.

Outside their home, the voices of the hmun rose in song, ushering out Fourth Minhal and welcoming First Par, the opening phase of each lunar cycle, and a fresh start to the calendar year. It was only a matter of hours before the first sliver of Ama's curious red eye would appear, and they would be safe.

But these were hours that the baby simply insisted on being present for. Lahni gritted her teeth, sweat stinging her eyes. Her mother-in-law, Euna Mi, patted her brow with a damp cloth, humming along with the hmun's song, calling forth Ama's return with more urgency than most.

"The Grand Ones would understand it's not our fault, wouldn't they?" Tonão Sol asked his mother, his voice wavering slightly. "She was planned for Hiwei, Par at the *earliest*—"

"She had plans of her own," Euna said, her eyes wrinkling at the corners with a smile.

"But they won't—I mean, they wouldn't exile us. They're—she's so early, it wasn't on purpose, it's the very last day!" Despite his best efforts, Tonão's conviction sounded a lot more like desperation. Lahni could hardly blame him; not two years earlier her neighbours, Esteona Nor's children, had been sent to their deaths with their Minhal child in their arms. For the good of everyone. For the safety of the hmun.

Her belly cramped and she squeezed her eyes shut, shaking with the effort of swallowing every last cry her throat begged to release.

May this pain make my child fierce, she thought. *May it make her survive. May it make her Par.*

"My son, now is not the time to worry," Euna Mi murmured, rubbing Lahni's belly to the rhythm of the new year's song. Lahni almost asked her to stop; they could not tempt the child out with joyful music, not into a world that would not want her.

"How—how long now?" Lahni asked, her legs trembling as her body betrayed her with every contraction. She lurched forward, a soft sob rising up from within her. "I can't, Mother Mi, I can't—"

"It seems like a very good time to worry, Mother—"

"Or perhaps," Euna Mi interrupted, her voice suddenly stone-solid, "it is a good time for you to catch." She fixed her son with a meaningful look, disregarding all confusion on his face and nodding to the kneeling point on the floor. "I'm in the other room, singing with your Viunwei while we pack his things. Otherwise, I would be here."

3

For a moment Lahni could only stare at her, dizzy as she grappled with the woman's intention. It was the role of grandparents to catch the baby, to have the wisdom of the elders cradle the first breath of the newborns—to pass the role off to her son would be nothing short of blasphemy. Unconventional as Euna Mi was—as all of the Mi phase children were known to be—she held substantial influence in the hmun. Her honesty was taken at face value. It would not be long before she would be called forth to take her Grand Ones' Vows, to sit upon the council as Grandmother Mi to the entire community. And yet here she was, breaking one of the laws it held most sacred.

Lahni opened her mouth, wanting to confirm, wanting to question, but then the baby was coming and she could do nothing but bite down on the rag that had dried out her tongue, succumbing to every signal her body had been throwing at her for the past several hours. With one firm pat on Tonão's shoulder, Euna Mi rose with the grace of a much younger woman, clapping her hands and erupting into song as she exited the room to find her grandson Viunwei.

It would have been easier on the young parents, to have another person there. But even Euna Mi could not be so brazen in the spiting of her gods.

The child entered the world to the sound of her father's singing, untroubled by the black sky blanketing the mountain. Gods or no, she would wail just the same. The moment Lahni recovered her breath she joined in the song, her rasped voice raised to fill all of the space she

4

had left empty in her labouring. Guided by love as much as fear, they filled their home with music, determined to cover the cries of the baby that had come too soon.

They sang the new year's hymn in familiar harmony, both privately wishing they could be singing their bawdy travel songs instead. Tonão rested his head on his wife's shoulder, singing louder when she could not find the energy—for once, she was the one who could not keep up with him. The baby latched onto her mother's breast, drinking up life as eagerly as any Par that ever was.

Except she wasn't.

When the songs of the village finally died down, the silence in the home of Lahni Par and Tonão Sol stretched on for miles. The neighbours had come back in next door, and Lahni could hear their words muffled through the stone walls, the clinking sounds of their packing for the crossing. Lahni held her breath and stroked the baby's head, willing her silent. Her bad luck, her birthright, would catch up the moment she started crying.

When the terrified hush was disturbed, it was by Euna Mi, whose eyes twinkled with her best imitation of surprise as she opened the door. "How marvellous!" she exclaimed, walking over to peer at the little bundle that was her second grandchild. Lahni could only watch, worn down from fear and effort. Beside her, Tonão did not dare to speak. "Your labour is picking up now, isn't it? How fortunate, to have this child on the opening day of First Par! What a bold traveller she will be, just like her mother, crawling down the side of the mountain before she can even walk!" Next door, the voices stopped. Euna turned her gaze to her son, raising her eyebrows.

"We are—we are very lucky," he said, his voice gone tight with the wavering strain of suppressed tears. "Very lucky, Mother."

"I'll share the news, I'll share the news! And then I'll be right back to you, so don't you worry about that," the woman chirped, stroking Lahni's hair with pride. "What a gift you've given me today, getting me out of my own packing duties to meet the second Par of the family! Though I cannot say the crossing will be much fun for you, Lahni my dear. We'll make sure you rest at each of the Fingers. Give that baby a good taste of sky."

"Rest would be good," Lahni said, not having to feign her fatigue in the slightest.

"But for now, you work." It was remarkable, how Euna Mi could greet misfortune with nothing but a familiar smile and tea on the fire. Perhaps it was the nature of her own birth phase that allowed her to abandon custom without a second thought. Perhaps it was the fierceness of her love. Whatever it was, Lahni did not argue. "Only a few hours now, I'd say. Not much longer at all."

In the earliest hours of First Par, the second child of Lahni Par and Tonão Sol was born a second time. Her mother yelled and groaned and her father wept, and both of them meant every last bit of it. Grandmother Mi caught the baby, passed from one adult to another, and welcomed her into the world with a sharp pinch on the thigh that moved her to wailing loud enough for the neighbours three houses down to hear. It was an unfair reward, for having been dutifully quiet following her first entry into the world. Lahni feared she might never let them live it down.

Together, Lahni and Tonão sat and looked upon their child. Such misfortune, saved only by luck and by heresy. This time, neither of them were singing.

"What do we name them?" Tonão asked softly, wiggling his little finger into the baby's angry fist.

"Her," she reminded him firmly. "Par." In naming the baby a child of Par, its gender had been determined feminine; an accidental misgendering was all it would take to raise suspicions about her being Minhal.

"Of course Par, my love, but—"

"I don't know, Ton," Lahni said with an exhausted laugh, gazing down at the child as if she might have some sort of insight to offer. All things considered, it wouldn't be surprising—the child had entered the world riding in on an unexpected choice. Unpredictability would likely to be a theme in the coming years. A troublesome baby for troublesome parents, eager to disrupt the tidy household they had established with Viunwei Soon. If she was ruled by Par, the conflict would serve holy purpose. If she was ruled by Minhal, then who was to say?

The fussy little bundle sighed in Lahni's arms, her soft new brow already creased with worry. She reached down, brushing it away with her thumb.

"Sohmeng," her husband said, leaning back against the hanging furs that insulated their cool walls.

"What?"

"Her name. Sohmeng." *She who becomes.* With all the odds stacked against her new daughter, Lahni figured it was a good place to start.

"Sohmeng Par," she said, and she knew with sudden certainty that there would be no other names up for consideration. Though she had never claimed to be any sort of oracle, Lahni Par knew some things like they had been carved into her bones: how to track and avoid the sãoni that roamed the forests below, what lullabies would soothe her son to sleep, her husband's favourite ways to be kissed, which lunar phases would deliver her safely from their own hmun, Ateng, to the many hmun down below in Eiji. And now, that this child would be marvellous and challenging and full of purpose.

What purpose that was remained to be seen. She would simply have to become.

Part One:
Ateng

ONE

ON THE LAST DAY OF HER LIFE inside the mountain, Sohmeng Par was fighting with her brother. Perhaps she would have done things differently if she knew what was coming, but the gods did not see fit to warn her, and she most likely would not have listened to them anyway.

"Sohmeng, I have never been so *humiliated*—"

Sohmeng tended to dig her heels in when she was being lectured, and no one exercised that skill quite like Viunwei. The current list of grievances included something about her being inconsiderate, something about her disrupting the whole community, something else along the lines of *a-new-low-even-for-you*. She wasn't really catching it all. In fact, for the most part, she was doing her best to tune it out, counting her steps as a helpful means of distracting herself from her brother's hysterics. If he was saying anything important, she figured it would be brought up again in this fight's inevitable reprise later that night.

"By the moons, you are making a *game* out of being

difficult," he hissed, storming behind her as she padded her way down the damp stairs into the cavern's throat, trying to outpace him.

"Am I winning?" she asked dryly.

"*Sohmeng Par.*"

"*Viunwei Soon!*"

It was going to be a long walk down to Chehangma's Gate.

She blew her bangs out of her face in an irritable huff, listening to the chittering of small creatures that clung to the walls high above, their blinking opalescent eyes illuminated by the glow of lichen and wovenstone. Sohmeng had half a mind to grab her knife and chip a chunk off the wall— her old dice were beginning to lose some of their lustre, and she was sick of squinting every time she wanted to cast them after everyone else had gone to bed. But making an unsanctioned cut in the mountain might actually kill Viunwei, and even she wasn't so bold as to desecrate the caves on the way to a meeting with the Grand Ones.

See? she thought, glaring up at the ceiling. *Not entirely inconsiderate.*

"What exactly are you planning on saying?" Viunwei asked tightly. For all he looked like their father, fair-eyed and unreasonably tall, his face lacked any of the man's easygoing nature. Under the soft green light of the wovenstone, the shadows even made him look cruel. "You've had this discussion with them time after time, you know as well as I do that they are not going to let a tengmun kar do the work of an adult. You're still a child, Sohmeng."

"It's not my fault that my Tengmunji was cancelled—" she began, unable to keep herself from rising to the bait.

"They won't care. No initiation, no opinion," he said, cutting her off with a dismissive shake of his head. "This is a bad choice. Go in, apologize for what you've done, and try to sound like you mean it. No special requests, no big ideas. Just be humble, for once in your life."

"Yes, oh mighty brother, beacon of stability, cleverest of them all!" She threw her hands into the air, giving him a scathing bow and nearly falling down the stairs in the process. He jumped to catch her, but she smacked his hands away. "I've listened to your advice. I've taken it into consideration. And I'm going to do this my way. If you don't like it, you can walk right back the way you came, but I am not putting up with your cosmically-ordained melodrama today."

She turned away before he could respond, stomping her way down the last of the stairs. The glow along the cave's walls grew brighter as the veins of wovenstone thickened, then dimmed once more as soft rays of sunlight shone into Fochão Dangde. That was the magic of Chehangma's Gate: a skylight in the mountain, welcoming the gift of the gods' direct gaze down upon the moons' eldest representatives. Sohmeng unclenched her fists and took a deep breath of the damp, musty air. Silently she named the phases in her head, searching for her best self in the rhythm of the cycle: *Par, Go, Hiwei, Fua, Tang, Sol, Jão, Pel, Dongi, Se, Won, Nor, Chisong, Heng, Li, Ginhãe, Mi, Ker, Hiun, Ãofe, Soon, Nai, Tos, Jeji, Minhal.*

Self-consciously, she combed through her thick hair with her fingers, as though she could mold her thoughts into something clever. It didn't matter how many times she had brought her troubles to the Grand Ones before, today could still be different. She would enter with peace. She would listen with humility. She would not be difficult. At the end of each argument, the Grand Ones always encouraged her to practice patience, to contain her reactions to the things she could not change.

The problem was, no one ever seemed to have any answers when she asked precisely how that was done.

Still trailing behind her, Viunwei had, remarkably, shut up for the time being. Squaring her shoulders, Sohmeng walked through the Gate, drilling the same idea into her head that she always did: *be better. Be something they won't hate. But be yourself, too.*

Maybe today would be the day those thoughts didn't spark off each other and ignite in disastrous flame.

Light wafted in hazy rays upon the greyed heads of the Grand Ones. Twenty-four elders sat around twenty-five spots in a circle, each perched on a stone seat with thick moss padding to cushion their aching backs and furs to keep their legs warm. At the base of each chair, the markings of their ruling lunar phases were engraved, matched with the tattoos that had been bestowed upon their cheeks when they were identified as Ateng's eldest living representative of that phase. The tattoos were a reminder of their twilight year purpose, to embody the most powerful lessons the moons had to offer.

Sohmeng did her best to enter quietly, not wanting to be overbold in her disruption of their low, creaking conversation. Of the twenty-four Grand Ones who had the power to determine her fate, she wasn't sure she could count ten whose good favour she was currently in. When Grandfather Se glanced at her with disinterest bordering on contempt, she felt her shoulders fall. Yet again she would have to rely on Grandmother Mi, who, as always, wore a look of faint amusement that showed off her missing tooth.

"Sohmeng Par," the woman said with a little hum. "I hear we've been having trouble with the children?"

Sohmeng lowered her chin respectfully and was about to address them properly when the sounds of Viunwei's footsteps quickly caught up with her. He stood beside her, eyes lowered, the perfect pained showcase of a shamed family member. She could have killed him right there, in full view of gods and Grand Ones alike.

"Yes, Grand Ones," she replied, doing her best to hide all nettling thoughts of fratricide. "I came to you as quickly as I could, hoping to explain myself—"

"And we are all so eager to hear today's explanation," Grandfather Se snorted, bringing his cup of mountain marrow up to his big, froglike mouth. A few of the Grand Ones chuckled at that, prompting a dismayed sigh from Viunwei. Sohmeng clenched her jaw.

"I lost my patience with the children today," she said, with great honesty and humility. "I'll be the first to admit it. What I said was—"

"'*Fine, don't take your bath. That's how sãoni like their little human snacks: pungent and savoury. I'm sure the stink of you will bring them right up into the mouth of the cave,*'" Grandmother Ginhãe said flatly. Sohmeng cringed. Out of the mouth of Grandmother Ginhãe, with her suspiciously perfect memory, there wasn't much Sohmeng could argue.

"... a little harsh," she hazarded, but after being met with the appalled looks of several Grand Ones, quickly amended to: "Completely out of line!"

The unhappy tisks she had come to expect were elevated to audible groaning. Beside her, Viunwei was wearing his *Soh-how-could-you* face so hard that she thought it might get stuck that way.

"Completely out of line," she repeated slowly, hoping she sounded like she believed it.

"And is there a *reason*," Grandfather Se asked, shifting in his chair with a grunt, "why you thought it was appropriate to frighten the children that you're supposed to be looking after, that you're supposed to be modelling good behaviour for, by suggesting they are *snacks* for the most vicious predators our hmun has ever known?"

"I guess I—I have a passion for hyperbole?" she suggested, prompting another wave of grumbling broken only by Grandmother Mi's loud guffaw. Despite the room's general aura of disapproval, Sohmeng was thankful for that laugh. She took a moment to gather herself as the rest of the Grand Ones got the murmuring and head-shaking out of their system. "Look, I know that I made a mistake today. A bad one. I'm short-tempered, I'm not good with kids—"

"We had hoped you might *learn* something from this role," offered gentle Grandfather Tang with a tired smile. "Particularly given the extra years that you have had to spend in it."

Sohmeng nearly laughed in his face at the suggestion that being indefinitely trapped in the role of a child could be anything other than stifling. She had lost every battle in the past where she'd begged to be allowed into adult roles despite not having completed her Tengmunji. Not like it was her fault—a surprise attack from the sãoni had doomed the last crossing the hmun ever attempted, destroying the Sky Bridge and any viable route to the twin mountain Sodão Dangde along with it.

She still remembered standing at the mouth of Fochão Dangde with the other batengmun, heart soaring as she prepared to at last have the space to grow up. And then, in a flurry of claws and shredded vines, it was gone.

She clenched her fists. As long as the Sky Bridge remained damaged and the crossing impossible, she would be refused access to the privileges of adulthood. And for as long as she was a tengmun kar, she—and the rest of those who missed their window with the fall of the Bridge—would be stuck in developmental limbo. Unable to move into their proper roles, unable to pursue relationships, unable to contribute their opinions on the workings of the hmun.

"I *have* learned from this, Grandfather Tang," she insisted, doing her best to control the bitterness creeping into her tone. "I've learned that I'm not—I'm not *meant* for the kind of work that's being given to me. I know you won't let me take on an adult role, that you'd be happy letting me stay a child until I'm dead as long as—" Viunwei cleared his throat loudly. She gritted her teeth and tried again. "There has to be some other role to put me in. This job isn't working for me. It was fun guiding the younger kids when I was also younger, but now it just—it isn't *working*. I know I can't be initiated until everyone can cross to Sodão Dangde, and that it might be a long time before that's possible. But in the meantime . . . I'm still going to be Par." The words were unsteady on her tongue, full of truth and complication. She couldn't think on them too long; it was easier to ride in on her instincts impulsively. "I'm going to be forward and curious and self-indulgent. I'm going to push back against what I don't like, and I'm going to do it loudly. And I know it might make things difficult in the hmun, but . . . even you can't change the minds of the moons. No matter how they speak to you."

It was a bold statement to make, as discerning as it was inflammatory. She could already see the ripple it created in the room, and read the reactions of the Grand Ones, as predictable as the phases themselves. Se, impatient with the individualistic thought. Mi, pleased by her approaching them with a new angle. Par, satisfied with the unfiltered honesty of a phase-mate. Tang, anxiously watching the way everyone's emotions squared and sparked. Ginhãe, reflecting on everything that had occurred up until this point. On and on—Sohmeng looked at each of them, searching for some sort of general consensus.

"What would you have us do?" asked Grand One Chisong. The rest of the Grand Ones turned to them, some humming softly in appreciation for the simplicity of their question; the insight of Chisong children was taken into double consideration, listened to with double thoughtfulness, for they held the full wisdom of the two moons Ama and Chehang combined. It was hard for Sohmeng to hold eye contact with them.

"I..." She hadn't actually thought that far ahead. But this was her chance to change something, and she wasn't about to miss it. "I was set to be a trader, like my parents. I remember what they used to tell me about the other hmun in the network. I know the legends of Polhmun Ão, and I speak Dulpongpa pretty well. I—I still practice it, even though there isn't much use for it anymore." It was oddly intimate, to admit her knowledge of the trade tongue. Something in Viunwei's shoulders softened, and she quickly forced herself to look back at Grand One Chisong, who despite everything was a more accessible presence than her brother. "I know I can't go for any sort of venture in Eiji, not with the sãoni still swarming the foot of the mountain. But there ... there has to be something I can do, something that makes use of my abilities. Something better than giving the youngest of the hmun nightmares."

Grand One Chisong smiled slightly at that, leaning back in their seat and looking to the rest of the Grand Ones, who began passing suggestions back and forth too quickly to keep up with. Sohmeng tried not to look too baffled that she was being given fair consideration.

To a point, of course. "Ridiculous," said Grandfather Se. "Absolutely ridiculous!"

"It wouldn't trouble anyone," retorted Grandmother Par. "You're resisting for the sake of being resistant!"

"Perhaps consulting the oracles would be wise?" offered Grandfather Sol.

"Ah, I am nearly out of marrow," said Grand One Hiun.

"Viunwei Soon," interjected Grandmother Mi loudly. "How many years have you seen now?"

The geriatric clamour abruptly stopped as the room's attention swerved to Viunwei, who seemed entirely unprepared to join the conversation.

"Nineteen," he answered with an uncertain frown.

"And you still collect eggs from the cliffside. Nearly six years out of your Tengmunji." Grandmother Mi shook her head at the rest of the Grand Ones. "Now that's a shame if I ever did see one. A boy like this, strong in the moons, withering in a transitory job."

"True enough," Grandfather Se said reluctantly. "He displayed remarkable leadership ability during his Tengmunji. All of his peers still seek his council."

"And look at his broad shoulders!" Grandmother Mi continued, untroubled by Viunwei's obvious discomfort. "The harness must cut terribly into his skin, and the rope strains. That sort of work was not made for a body so far grown. The smaller of the collectors continue to do their jobs admirably, but I fear we may begin seeing accidents the longer we keep them up there. There's a reason this job is meant for those in transition. The oja beans too long on the stalk grow bitter."

There were murmurs among the Grand Ones as tension spread through the room. This was a truth that was rarely acknowledged within the hmun these days: the impact of a disrupted Tengmunji reached farther than the belligerent Sohmeng Par. It was a symbol of all of the problems that had grown since the Sky Bridge fell. No matter the adjustments that had been put in place for the hmun to continue to thrive in its day-to-day life, the long-term consequences of so many people being trapped in one mountain were impossible to avoid—particularly when seeking resources on the ground below was no longer an option. No matter how strict the will of the gods, devotion could not outlast starvation. While the hmun had found ways to navigate around Ateng's currently-limited agricultural prospects, they wouldn't hold forever.

Sohmeng shifted her footing, sending up Par-shaped prayers. Everyone could call her selfish if they wanted; it was true. But there were more reasons to allow her to move forward uninitiated than simply appeasing her own desires.

Grand One Chisong hushed the circle with a raised hand, turning their attention back to Sohmeng. For all they were frighteningly incisive, there was also something sympathetic in their dark eyes. Perhaps it was because they were the youngest of the Grand Ones; maybe they had forty years on Sohmeng, but it certainly brought them closer to understanding her than the octogenarians. And she had to consider the complementary nature of their beings: two full gods' eyes, contrasted with—

She lowered her gaze once more. Across the room, the seat of Minhal sat empty as it ever had.

"We have never crossed this boundary," Grand One Chisong said at last. "Many of us are wary, as we should be. In times as precarious as these, it is dangerous to move against the will of the gods. But also, we must consider the more material dangers of our current situation. We can not, and should not, uproot the ways of our hmun all at once, but perhaps we can find compromises for the time being. Test the waters of the acceptability of diverging from the path we are comfortable with." Sohmeng nearly collapsed to the floor in gratitude. "We do not need to bring all of the batengmun kar into transitory work—in this time of Second Won, I think it would be wise to act only with great intention on matters that impact the future of Ateng as a whole. Nothing rushed, but no time wasted. Would you agree with my interpretation, Grandmother Won?"

Grandmother Won nodded, and many around them seemed satisfied. Grandmother Mi beamed at Sohmeng, happily tapping her finger against her cup of mountain marrow.

"Perhaps a vote, then," Grand One Chisong said. "Shall we allow Sohmeng Par to take Viunwei Soon's place collecting eggs from the mountainside, while we move him into work more suited to his capabilities?"

One by one the Grand Ones went in a circle, either raising a cup of mountain marrow in favour or keeping it in their laps. For some the answer was quick, marrow lifted fast enough to spill or an expression of distaste firm enough to make their thoughts on the matter clear. For others, there was a good deal of deliberation, punctuated by thoughtful sips of Fochão Dangde's lifeforce.

After raising his hand Grandfather Tang cleared his throat, giving Viunwei a look that Sohmeng didn't quite follow. "Perhaps, should this proposal pass, it would be a good time for Viunwei Soon to consider the advice of the oracles. Particularly as he moves fully into the role of a man." Viunwei simply nodded, his face betraying nothing of his feelings. His hands were white-knuckled at his sides.

Sohmeng watched the Grand Ones without breathing, waiting and wishing and wanting. And then it was done, fifteen votes to nine. With something simple as a roomful of raised cups, her life had changed.

"Sohmeng Par," said Grand One Chisong, bringing their mountain marrow down to their lips. "You have asked after your own destiny, and we have heard you out. As you can see, this decision was by no means easy, nor unanimous. Should the gods grant us a sign that this was an inauspicious choice, or should you do anything that suggests you are not ready for the responsibility you seek, we will not hesitate to take away this privilege." Sohmeng nodded furiously, not daring to speak. With her luck, this would be the moment her mouth would fire off something entirely inappropriate.

"Congratulations dear," Grandmother Mi said, unabashedly showing off her bias for her blood relation. "You've taken the first step out of your adolescence."

"So act like it, girl." Grandmother Par looked down her long nose at Sohmeng. "Cut through the tangled path, don't burn it down."

Sohmeng lifted her chin, unafraid of the heavy expectations that had been suddenly placed upon her shoulders. This was what she had asked for. "Thank you, Grand Ones," she said, bowing so low that something popped in her back. "Their watchful eyes upon you."

"Their watchful eyes upon you," the Grand Ones echoed, and Sohmeng knew she was dismissed.

Two

THAT NIGHT, by the dimming light of their home's small hearth, Sohmeng quickly realized that she wasn't going to have much of an opportunity to celebrate her victory. Grandmother Mi's knees had forced her to stay the night at Chehangma's Gate with the rest of the Grand Ones who were too frail to make the challenging journey up and down the stairwell, leaving Sohmeng trapped alone with Young Grandfather Passive-Aggression himself.

Viunwei had hardly spoken a word to her since they got home, but the aggrieved clanking of his spoon against his dinner bowl was a monologue unto itself. She scooped up a roasted fiddlehead, refusing to indulge his sulking. As the Grand Ones had once said, being upset did not require her to react. She could be serene in the face of anger.

"Just because you got your way today doesn't mean that what you said to those children was acceptable," he suddenly said, launching Sohmeng out of her serenity and straight into a reaction.

"Oh godless—sorry, what's that?" she asked, cupping a hand to her ear. "'*Congratulations Sohmeng on something you've wanted for ages finally happening! I know it means a lot to you, and I want to show my support as your only brother!*' Wow, thanks Viunwei! It's great to know that under that stuck-up, unlikeable exterior, you really do care!"

"Sohmeng." Her name was like an insult on his tongue. "This isn't funny."

"No, I'm being serious!" she continued, stuffing a fiddle-head into her mouth. "The depths of your compassion are vast, and not to be underestimated."

"*Sohmeng.*" She jumped at the intensity of his voice, then scowled, swallowing. She wasn't about to back down from his judgement, but neither was she in the mood to test the limits of his patience. Viunwei was born under Third Soon, full of inner conflict and potential energy. As likely to make hard choices for the hmun as he was to create the need for them. It was almost funny to think that he had been planned to rein in their parents' overly-free spirits; when it came down to it, a Soon could be even more destructive than a Par. And yet, all his brooding ever seemed to inspire in others was respect. So thoughtful, so considerate.

It made Sohmeng hate him, just a little bit.

"You cannot make jokes about the children of the hmun getting eaten by sãoni," he said quietly. "I know you laugh at the things that upset you. You've said before that it . . . helps you." She was surprised that he remembered that much, and almost felt grateful when— "But it doesn't help other people. And considering what everyone in this hmun has been through, what our own family has lost, it's atrocious that you would say such a thing in response to something as trivial as your being annoyed."

Sohmeng's cheeks went hot. She knew he had a point. The moment the words were out, she knew that she had crossed a line. But all she had done was run her mouth, and now she was being treated like she'd hurled one of the kids off the mountain. Why was he judging her whole personality based on one mistake?

She scoffed, refusing to give him the apology he was fishing for. "Well thank you for the opinion I definitely didn't ask for. Oh, and while we're here, thank you for following me down to Chehangma's Gate!" Viunwei opened his mouth to argue anew, but Sohmeng cut him off, raising her voice. "No! I knew I made a mistake, and I was trying to handle it myself. But you followed me anyway because you were so bent on making me look like a child!"

"I followed you because I couldn't trust that you wouldn't—!" Through the walls, the distinct sounds of their neighbours' voices could be heard. Viunwei paused, clearing his throat. "...wouldn't make things worse."

"I did fine without you," she replied coldly, putting down her empty dinner bowl. "If you were actually paying attention rather than dancing to the tune of your own self-importance, you might have even noticed that they gave me what I asked for."

Viunwei threw his hands in the air, making an exasperated sound that reminded Sohmeng of their mother. She jabbed at the fire with the poker as if it could smother the thought before it blossomed into anything more painful.

"When you act out, it reflects on all of us, Sohmeng."

"Reflects on you, you mean," she muttered.

"Yes," he said, his matter-of-factness hurting in a new and unexpected way. "It reflects poorly on me."

Par that she was supposed to be, it should have been a relief to be faced with such directness. It should have been better than the way he kept her at a distance when they were in public together, or quickly spoke over her when she challenged someone. She had tried for so long to get something honest out of him that she had managed to fool herself into believing that when it finally came, it would be something kind.

After all, there wasn't really anyone else left to be her friend.

It was getting hard to remember the last time she had been welcomed by the other batengmun kar. They had stuck together for a while after their failed Tengmunji, mourning their collective loss and searching for closeness in the small community they should have been. But then Sohmeng asked too many questions. Sohmeng complained too much. Sohmeng was a bad influence. What began as her friends avoiding her turned into a series of outright communication bans from the Grand Ones: if she was going to argue about the rules, she wasn't going to spread discontent to the others.

She still wondered if any of them had defended her, if any of them had considered her friendship worth the risk of disappointing the hmun.

"Am I really that embarrassing to you?" she asked, watching sparks pop from the end of the poker. "Am I that bad?"

"Sohmeng," Viunwei began, putting down his food.

"Really," she asked again, a short laugh scratching her throat. "Is it truly so shameful to call me your sister? Am I that difficult for you to love?"

"That's not—"

"Because with the way you talk to me," she continued, raising her voice even as it shook, "sometimes I wonder if you wish I'd just been ex—"

"Soh!" Viunwei shouted, and the fear in his voice startled the fight out of both of them. Sohmeng could hear the blood pounding in her ears, feel how clammy her hands had gotten from approaching that which was not spoken of in their house. Viunwei stared at her, rattled, and Sohmeng shook herself out of her own shock, doing her best to put on an air of familiar annoyance. Silence passed between them, waning from pained to uncomfortable to awkward.

Viunwei cleared his throat, rubbing his nose self-consciously. For a moment Sohmeng saw something change in him, a certain hunch in the shoulders that brought back memories of the nervous, serious boy her brother had been as a child. "That's not," he began, unable to meet her eye as his expression shifted, bizarrely, to embarrassment. "Sohmeng, it's not that I—I just, I'm trying to court someone, alright?" He spat out the last words as though he'd accidentally swallowed a moth.

"…What?" She blinked, straightening up. "Wait, what?"

"I said I'm trying to court someone," he mumbled, suddenly very interested in his meal.

"Who?"

"Femi Hiun."

"*Femi?*" Sohmeng stifled a snort as he went to shush her. "The same Femi who used to cry when we were kids because they thought the mountain would melt when it rained?"

"Stop that. They're perfectly nice—"

"Can I give them rainwater as a wedding gift?"

"Sohmeng!" Despite his best attempts to scold, laughter tinged his voice. It made Sohmeng's spine soften where she had gone all jagged inside, made her heart come unstuck from itself. "No, you absolutely cannot do that. Besides, we don't even know if their family will consent to the marriage."

Realization settled in Sohmeng's gut like a stone in the soup. She thought of this morning's antics with the children, of the distance the rest of the batengmun kar kept from her, the day she tossed the neighbour's washing down the well, the time she punched a boy at the dance in an attempt to teach him a lesson about self-confidence. She thought of the judgemental way her brother looked at her after each of these incidents, and felt a twisting in her chest as the distance between them suddenly made more sense. Regardless of how justified she felt in her actions, she probably wasn't a shining example of a sister-in-law.

Sohmeng wanted to apologize. She really did. But when

she opened her mouth what came out instead was, "Why Femi? I don't think I've ever heard you speak a word about them until now."

"The oracles approached me," Viunwei said, resting his chin on one of his knees. "They thought a marriage between a Soon and a Hiun would be spiritually auspicious for the hmun. The Grand Ones think highly of what our children could be like."

Sohmeng wrinkled her nose, looking at her brother and trying to imagine him as a father. It was hard enough to imagine him as the leader everyone was always making him out to be—apparently there was a lot she didn't know about him. Still, what she *did* know didn't line up. "What about Jinho Tang?" she asked.

"What about him?" Viunwei's voice tightened like a spike had gone through his foot and he was trying very hard not to acknowledge it.

"What *about* him?" Sohmeng echoed, laughing. "I mean you two have only been circling each other since before your Tengmunji. I figured if you were formally courting anyone, it would be him."

"It isn't—it isn't as strong of a match," he said, a little too quickly. "And seeing as we're both male we'd have to navigate a damwei to carry our children, which adds a whole new element to determining our phasal compatibilities, and there wouldn't even be a guarantee that they would turn out how the oracles are hoping, so ..."

As he trailed off, Sohmeng couldn't help but notice how rehearsed the words sounded, like the kind of internal monologue someone runs through their head over and over when they can't sleep. Championing something they don't believe in. Sohmeng knew the feeling well, but she was startled to see it in her brother, who always presented as so self-assured. He could be a lot of things—difficult and stubborn, unbelievably volatile beneath all of his performed stability, the slick shard of a red moon lurking below the calm of a swollen white. But this was different.

And as soon as she saw it for the pain that it was, it was gone, stuffed back below his composed exterior. "We need to think about the future of the hmun," he said firmly. "There are more important things than our own wants. If Jinho is reasonable, he'll understand."

Sohmeng put her bowl aside, speaking as cautiously as she knew how. "Reasonable or not, he's a person. No one wants to be tossed aside."

"I'm not tossing him aside."

"But you kind of are, Viunwei," Sohmeng sighed, scratching her head where her bun had come loose. "I get it. It sounds like the Grand Ones are putting a lot of pressure on you. But even if it is for the hmun, he's still going to be hurt if—"

"I don't remember asking you for advice on this," Viunwei snapped, clearing both of their dishes with a clatter. Sohmeng groaned softly, leaning her head back against the wall with a thud. "And I don't know what a tengmun kar would know about courting, anyway."

The words stuck on Sohmeng like an insect's barbs,

clinging and repellant all in one. For once, she didn't much feel like pulling them out and opening the wound any further, so she held her tongue as he stormed off.

She supposed that's what she got for expecting that things might go differently, for imagining that Viunwei was actually going to treat her like an equal. They had cycled through this back-and-forth with all the consistency of the moons, and it always ended up the same: because she hadn't completed her Tengmunji, she would always be denied a voice. She was too old for a child's careless freedom, but too young on a technicality for the responsibilities of an adult. Even the promise of a new world opening tomorrow wasn't balm enough for the years of chafing anger that had built up.

How many times had she fallen into daydreams about what her Tengmunji should have been? The lowering of the Sky Bridge's rope, the lighting of the Batengmun's Lantern, the last look at the hmun making its biennial pilgrimage, leaving her and the rest of the batengmun behind to find their way into adulthood. She had seen it from the other side seven times over, ever-impatient for her turn.

She supposed she should be thankful that she was too young for the last Tengmunji. Better to be with the hmun than trapped alone with the fall of the Sky Bridge.

Right?

"I'm going to bed." Viunwei's voice, softened from the other room, still hardened from his anger, pulled Sohmeng back to herself. Back to the cool floor of their empty home, the great lonely quiet of their too-large shared space. "You should, too. Tomorrow won't be easy."

Sohmeng took out her bun, letting her dark hair tumble down to her shoulders in a thick tangle. Tomorrow she would walk along the outside of the mountain, feast her eyes on the expanse of Eiji's jungle, on the mountains curved like the hipbones of the gods. It had been years since she last laid eyes on the fullness of the lost territories. A different cycle. A different life.

"Goodnight, Sohmeng," Viunwei called, and something like regret lingered on the edges of his words. Sohmeng said nothing, taking her dice from her pocket and retreating to her room.

THREE

SOHMENG WASN'T SURE which came first: the ringing of the morning bells or the opening of her eyes. Sleep had come in restless fits and bursts, her body jittery with anticipation that had carried through to the morning. The only proof that she had dozed at all was the gentle ache where her dice pressed into her closed fist—she must have drifted off while fidgeting with them.

She rose and splashed her face with water before rinsing her bangs and giving them a good fluff with her fingers. As she chewed on a stalk of lemongrass to get the morning taste out of her mouth, she heard Viunwei getting ready in the next room. It struck her that his life would be changing as much as her own today; she wondered how he was feeling about it.

Her answer came in the form of a loud clatter of a falling vanity bowl, followed by a muffled curse. It seemed that anxiety was on the agenda for this morning.

Sohmeng picked at a piece of lemongrass caught in the

gap between her front teeth, considering. Checking on Viunwei was the kind thing to do, especially given how last night had played out. They could go to breakfast together, put on the performance of a stable and supportive family.

Another noise came from his room, the familiar sound of a head banging into the too-sloped roof and the substantially louder curse that followed. Sending out a silent apology to whatever of her parents remained in the house, Sohmeng grabbed her bowl and slipped quickly out the door. After all, today was something to be celebrated: no more babysitting! No more miserable, menial tasks! This was the first day of her adult life, and she wasn't going to let it be spoiled by one of Viunwei's moods.

The main hall was busy with the morning rush of the hmun, families gathered around small fires, cooking and sharing their portions of the communal breakfast. The mountain's harvest had been strong for the past week, which made for larger portions, and a satisfied air hummed across the room as people doled out boiled eggs, dried fruit, and steaming, meaty mushrooms in rich dark sauce. She held her bowl out to be filled by one of the neighbours, thanking him graciously, and even more graciously ignoring the cocked eyebrow he gave in response as she happily made her way to an empty table. Knowing what was to come today, she didn't even feel lonely.

I can totally do this, she thought, looking around with no small amount of smugness at the main hall. *None of them have any idea, but today I'm going prove just how capable I am.*

As she dug into her mushrooms, a warm voice spoke from behind her: "'And how the sky cleared for the people of The Last City of Polhmun Ão, and they danced in the streets as though they had embers between their toes!'" Before the line was even finished, Sohmeng was grinning, and she turned to face her Grandmother Mi.

"'And the gods looked down upon them with gratitude, for they could see their children were ready, at last, to receive their divine knowledge,'" Sohmeng recited back with ease—the epic of Polhmun Ão had been one of her staple bedtime stories. Re-enacting her favourite parts with the children she watched was one of the only good parts of her job—her *former* job, she remembered with another grin.

Grandmother Mi tugged on Sohmeng's ear with a mischievous smile and took the seat beside her. "You are glowing, my Sohmeng. Bright as any moon."

"I can't believe it's finally happening. It's been so long, I was starting to think that I would never . . ." she trailed off, embarrassed to be admitting her fears aloud.

"'Never' is a lazy word," Grandmother Mi tutted, patting her granddaughter's leg. "A lazy word for unimaginative people."

"Like Viunwei?" Sohmeng sniped in spite of herself, popping another mushroom in her mouth.

Her grandmother hummed a sound that could have been a laugh if it wasn't so tired. "Viunwei is more imaginative than you think, my girl. It is what makes him so terribly afraid. Your Damdão Kelho was like that too, do

37

you remember? Too clever for his own good; it bled into all his caring."

That was true enough—Rikelho Fua had always been the fussiest of her parental figures. Her parents had both been born female, and Rikelho had taken the role of damwei, her and Viunwei's biological father, providing the necessities for a baby and extra grounding energy from the white moon Chehang to balance out Lahni's Par influence. He had never settled in a family of his own, and had often looked after her and Viunwei when their parents descended the mountain for trading. She still missed him, sometimes. She missed all of them.

"Sohmeng," Grandmother Mi said, shaking her from the memory, "despite our greatest wishes and best intentions, we all build our own nevers in this life. Even me. Today, when you look upon Eiji, face your nevers with courage, and they will yield to you."

"I . . . thank you, Grandmother Mi." Sohmeng wasn't sure what to make of that. The words seemed nearly premonitory, heavy in the air around the popping lightness of her eagerness. But before she could investigate them further, the second bells rang, calling the hmun to the dais for morning announcements.

"Oh my creaking knees, is that the time?" Grandmother Mi lifted herself with a grunt. "That old canker sore Ginhãe will never let me hear the end of it if I'm late. I'll see you tonight, my Sohmeng."

The old woman made her way to where all of the most mobile Grand Ones were seated, and Sohmeng scarfed down her breakfast and went to join the gathering throng of the hmun.

In truth, she only half-listened to the first portion of the announcements as she gnawed at a dried apricot. Lunar reports, general notes about hmun cooperation, birthdays—it was the assignment changes she was really here for. Sure, she knew about the oncoming shift in her role, but the rest of the hmun didn't, and she was dying to see the looks on their faces. Troublesome Sohmeng Par, noticed at last for her ingenuity. This was better than her first sixteen birthdays combined.

She glanced around the room for the other batengmun kar, wondering how they might react to the announcement, if they would say anything to her at all. Not that she cared—if they wanted to avoid her for the sake of sucking up to the Grand Ones, that was their problem. But her advocating for this change could impact all of their futures. Maybe this would change something. Maybe they would sit with her again at breakfast.

As one of the oracles was stepping up to say something about Ama's influence on the week's labour division, Viunwei arrived by her side. He stared up at the dais, brow creased with severity, eyes as anxious as she had ever seen them. She looked away with a scowl—was he seriously playing chaperone for her *again*? Now, of all times?

"We have some assignment changes for this morning," called one of the leaders. "Please listen closely for your names ..."

"Sohmeng," Viunwei said softly, then hesitated. Frankly,

she was astounded that he would dare to interrupt the riveting once-in-a-morning opportunity to listen to announcements.

"What?" she said, not looking at him.

"I—" he cut himself off, hesitating again, then tried to take her hand in an uncharacteristically tender gesture. She shook it off with a scoff, trying to figure out what had been done to the standoffish prince who was her brother.

"What's your problem?" she hissed. One of the people beside her glanced over, and she rolled her eyes.

"About last night—"

"Viunwei Soon," called the announcer. "You will be shadowing Tsatong Soon, alongside the other coordinators. Please report to him for your assignment."

A soft murmur rippled the crowd, eyes falling on Viunwei. He broke his gaze from Sohmeng, bowing his head in respectful gratitude, and walked to his assigned mentor. A prestigious role to begin in, obviously. Sohmeng took a deep breath, pushing back the uncertainty that had bubbled up with her brother's attempt at what might have been reconciliation.

Talk about bad timing, she thought. *Some Soon you are.*

"Sohmeng Par," the announcer continued. Sohmeng's head shot up, her heart lifted— "please report to the north entrance of the main hall."

Sohmeng had to clench her jaw to keep it from dropping to the floor. Was it so much to ask for just a touch of recognition? Shoulders slumped, she manoeuvred her way through the crowd, doing her best to look appreciative.

Beneath the entrance to the north wing of the caves, she saw none other than Jinho Tang waving to her with climbing equipment slung over his shoulder. She couldn't help but feel awkward as she made her way over, the long-time familiarity between them tainted by her knowledge of how Viunwei was behaving.

"Hey, Jinho," she began, peering behind him to see if anyone else was waiting for her. "I was just ..."

"Looking for me, actually!" Jinho smiled warmly, wrapping his hands in waxed grip fabric. "I'll be training you today. Many congratulations on inheriting Viunwei's spot. You must be really excited."

"Oh! Thank you," she replied, grateful for the sympathetic nod he gave her, for the enthusiastic energy that radiated from him as though the celebration was his own. "I really—I really am."

"Then let's get you ready, yeah? Before the nerves kick in. Don't look at me like that, it happens to everyone." He hefted the supplies more comfortably onto his shoulder before starting up the stairwell carved into the mountain's interior.

"Not to me," Sohmeng said to herself, breathless with excitement as she ran up after him.

As they made the ascent, Sohmeng considered that her initial self-assessment might have been a little ambitious. Each step brought her higher up the mountain than she had ever been before, higher even than the point of the Sky Bridge's crossing. She tilted her head back, catching sight of the sunlight that streamed through an opening in the mountain's face, where small birds darted in and out in a rush of wings and trills. The stairs leveled out into an open cave, and the rays brightened into a full-on shine that lit the cave beyond the need for wovenstone.

"Best to keep back from the mouth," cautioned Jinho. "Your eyes need a minute to adjust, or you'll spend the first hour outside squeezing them shut."

"Right," nodded Sohmeng, as though seconds ago she had not been bracing to run directly to the entryway.

Jinho put down the gear, laying out all of the components for Sohmeng to see. She forced her gaze away from the shock of blue that teased just around the corner, attending instead to the information she needed if she wanted to survive her first day as an adult.

"Okay!" Jinho said brightly, pushing his hair back from his face. "Let's learn how not to fall off a mountain."

First he showed her the many straps on the harness, laughing at the way she blanched when she realized just how thin her lifeline to the mountain actually was. For all he talked about weight and counterweight and *a-long-practiced-method*, it looked a whole lot to Sohmeng like a big heap of rope. "It's a matter of where you fix your weight," he patiently explained for the third time, tightening the straps at her hips. Sohmeng thanked the gods and her mother for her thick thighs, her full waistline—she had no idea how the skinny collectors did this job without cushion. "As long as you keep yourself balanced and communicate with me, there shouldn't be any problems." For her own sake, she decided not to ask what a 'problem' entailed.

Once they made it to the mouth of the cave, which Jinho insisted she keep her back to, he introduced her to the pulley system they used, and taught her the hand gestures to signal the operators if her location needed to be adjusted beyond her basic range of movement. From there, she would use her feet to glide and hop along the cliff-face, reaching into the holes where the nests were and searching for eggs to place into the baskets attached at her thighs.

"Doesn't it bother the birds?" she asked, flexing her fingers in her new waxed wraps as the operator, Pasme Ker, locked her harness into place.

"The yellowbills? Oh, yeah, they hate it," Jinho said, nodding. "We plan our foraging for when they're out hunting. If any of them stay behind, a good shout usually scares them, but we've all been pecked once or twice." He held out an arm, showing off a small scar. "Most of the yellowbills have about three to four clutches a cycle, so you don't need to feel too bad about what you take."

"I didn't realize I was supposed to feel bad," she mused.

"Aaand that's why you're Par and I'm Tang," Jinho said with a laugh, squinting slightly as he peered out the mouth of the cave. "Speaking of, I guess it's time to find out if it's really true."

"If what's true?" she asked, anxious hope pressing against her ribs. If she was ready to be an adult? If she was deserving of this gift? If she was bound to mess it up?

"If you can literally only listen when your life depends on it."

To her surprise, Sohmeng found herself grateful for one last opportunity to be a little sister. "You're an *ass*," she began, grinning, but then Pasme was nudging her to go, and the sun was warm on her neck as she stepped backward into full view of clouds and birds and gods alike.

Four

THE DESCENT OVER THE SIDE of the cliff was possibly the most terrifying moment of Sohmeng's life. The world warped around her as she was liberated from solid ground, her feet scrabbling at the rough edges of the cliffside in toe-scraping reflex. She could feel her heartbeat in her tongue as clearly as the harness biting into her waist. All the while, Jinho called reassurances from above as he made his own exit. Distantly, she heard him say something about it being totally normal for new collectors to vomit on their first descent, but she was too busy trying not to prove him right to respond. She dared to look down—and then frantically grasped at the hanging rope with shaking hands, uncontrollable laughter rattling her jaw as she squeezed her eyes shut.

There came a faint whirring sound, and then Jinho was beside her, his voice moving in gentle tones. "Easy there, take your time," he said. She planted her feet more firmly against the cliff, and felt something tickle at her

45

ankle. Startled, she opened her eyes to see moss, bright green moss against sun-bleached sandstone, alive and thriving on the forehead of Fochão Dangde. Such a small thing, but bold enough to face down Chehangma the sun, the combined power of Ama and Chehang, piercing as a spear and all-warming as an embrace.

She turned to Jinho, eyes wide with wonder despite the way they ached in the brightness, and he laughed in delight, turning his body to the valley behind, below. And though her hands still shook, she mimicked his motion and faced the world she was estranged from.

The treetops were like a pot at full boil, rising and falling with mists roaming like steam. The Ãotul River and its many tributaries snaked along the ground, waters of the purest blue curling through mountains which rose in towers all across the land. It took her a moment to realize that the shapes darting in and out of the jungle were enormous birds in magnificent shades of magenta and turquoise and gold, that the music echoing in the clouds was their call and response. She released her grip on the rope, letting her fingers brush the mountain, tangling with sturdy flowering vines. Without regular exposure, it was easy to forget the breadth of Eiji.

"The view of the gods," murmured Jinho. The look on his face was akin to longing. "It still takes the breath from me. Every time."

Being a hmun of cave dwellers, many of her people dreaded this transitory job. It took a rare sort to gain pleasure from dangling from a rope miles above solid ground, but based on the way he sighed as he swung lightly in his harness, Jinho seemed to be one of them. What would happen, Sohmeng wondered, when he, like Viunwei, was moved into the job of a man? Would he be allowed to continue training the new collectors, or would he be forced back into the caves, away from the sunlight and the open air?

Her stomach knotted with guilt. She forced her gaze back to the land, searching for the sights she remembered from back when the hmun still made its crossing. There was the First Finger: a slim mountain in the cluster of three between Fochão and Sodão Dangde, each stable enough to serve as a pausing point during the crossing but not robust enough to live inside. Together, the range of five mountains sprawled high above the valley, the spread fingers of a hand raised in supplication to the gods' eyes, home to one hmun of many. Ateng.

Strange vines dangled from the First Finger, limp and ragged compared to the rest of the life speckling the mountains. With a lurch of dizziness, Sohmeng recognized them as the remains of the Sky Bridge, tattered but still hanging, a firm reminder of the darkest day in the hmun's history. It had been First Par, her fourteenth birthday, when the reptilian predators known as sãoni suddenly swarmed Fochão Dangde, shredding through the Sky Bridge and sending dozens of people to their deaths mid-crossing. For months after, she'd flinch at the sound of rope being cut, no matter how benign the context.

She steadied herself, facing the corpse of the Bridge like an opponent, like a Grand One, with reverence and respect and challenge. She tried to push down thoughts of the sãoni below, kept back only by the hmun's warriors stationed at the lower entryway, warding the creatures off with the silvertongue plant which was toxic to them.

The world she knew was such a fragile thing, bound together with nothing but sour leaves and human tenacity.

"Sohmeng?" Jinho asked, breaking her uneasy trance. "You alright?"

She turned to him and swallowed, finding the voice that the world had taken from her. "Yeah—I'm, I'm okay. Thanks for giving me a minute to ..." She laughed a little, gesturing to their surroundings. The harness swayed slightly and her hands shot back to the mountain.

"It gets easier," he smiled, tousling her hair and turning back to face the cliff. Sohmeng followed suit, blowing her bangs out of her eyes.

As she focused on the process of digging through the yellowbill nests, following Jinho's tips and encouragements, Sohmeng found that he was right. Keeping her attention on the repetitive motions allowed the dangerous and staggering nature of her task to settle into the back of her mind. Incredible, how even something as mythic as this could fall into a routine.

"Are any of the others coming out today?" she asked.

Jinho shook his head, lowering himself slightly to investigate a small, mossy cranny. "The Grand Ones thought your training might be easier without any distractions."

"Distractions," Sohmeng repeated, scowling as she stretched her arm into a nest. Of course the Grand Ones would warn Jinho about all the trouble she was just waiting to cause. "Good to know they have faith in me."

"Well it, it *is* a big day for you," Jinho attempted carefully, non-confrontational as any good Tang. "I'm sure they just wanted to make sure it went well."

"Yeah," Sohmeng snorted, "and Viunwei has been a nightmare since last night because he really cares, not because—agh!" She yanked her hand back, shaking it out and peering into the nest to see a fat, satisfied-looking beetle clicking its pincers.

"Bird or beetle?" Jinho called, placing two shining eggs into his basket before rising back up to meet her.

Embarrassed, Sohmeng lifted higher. "Beetle. Big blue one with a stupid, sharp mustache." She stepped to the left, pretending to search for a new nest.

He hummed sympathetically. "Fool's Gems. Nasty things." After a moment, he cleared his throat, speaking with the same caution as before. "Viunwei does care about you, you know. He's not great at showing it sometimes, but he loves you."

Suddenly remembering precisely who she was talking to, Sohmeng realized, like an idiot, what a huge opportunity she had here.

She considered what it would be like to have Jinho as an in-law. He mellowed out Viunwei a lot, and he was funny, and even though he didn't always say what he meant, his heart was in the right place. Maybe their relationship trouble wasn't her business, but Jinho sort of qualified as her friend and Viunwei definitely qualified as her brother . . .

. . . so it sort of *was* her business actually.

"Listen, Jinho . . ." she began, watching him smile as he pulled a large egg from a nest nearby. "You know Viunwei is like, totally in love with you, right?" The egg went crashing down onto the sãoni warriors stationed below. They yelled something up at Jinho and he shouted back a flustered apology. "I mean, he's a total moron for dumping you but—"

"Sohmeng, that's not really—"

"It's okay, you can say it! I won't be mad, I *agree* that he's the worst. Honestly, you deserve some sort of prize for willingly dating him."

"Sohmeng, I don't know how comfortable I am having this conversation with you," Jinho said, focusing intently on reaching for another egg.

"Yeah, yeah, I know, but listen," she continued, pulleying herself higher as she spotted a thin opening above. "I really like you, and I know Viunwei does, too. Obviously like, in a different way. I mean, you're a great guy, but *definitely* not my type—" The plain horror on Jinho's face shut her up. ". . . right. No. That was weird. What I'm *trying* to say is I really think the two of you can work things out if you just put in the effort."

"You can tell that to your brother, not me," Jinho suddenly snapped. The moment the words were out he shook his head, raising his hands. "No, no. I'm sorry

50

Sohmeng, that wasn't—I'm not dragging you into this."

Sohmeng was pretty sure she was the one who'd dragged Jinho into the conversation, but she'd take what she could get to avoid getting accused of being nosy. As she was planning her next move, something caught the sunlight in the nest above her. She squinted, trying to make out the shape, but all she could see was the glint of it, bright and flickering like nothing else on the face of the cliffs. She raised herself on the pulley once more, climbing to the edge of her range before the rope started to tug taut.

"Really," Jinho continued, "I shouldn't have said that, it's not fair of me to—Sohmeng, what are you doing?"

"Don't you see that?" she asked, spreading her toes to get a better grip as she climbed.

"See what?"

"Up there, that...that bright thing!" Her rope stretched above her, curving out of the mouth of the cave and around the cliff-face. "There, in the light!" She eyed the mountain, mapping her handholds, doubtful that the pulley operator could get her that far. Maybe it was difficult, but Jinho had already showed her how many precautions they had in place, and it would be worth it to bring something special back from her first day out. A good omen. She grabbed hold of one of the rocks, tugging herself up.

"I, I think so? But Sohmeng, be careful," called Jinho, abandoning his current nest to follow her. "Come back down, the rocks are jagged there—you don't want your rope grating against them."

Sohmeng grunted, letting her rope slacken slightly, using the strength of her body instead. Months of baby-sitting hadn't done much for her triceps. "Look, I can release some of the pressure, and I've almost . . . got it . . ." She stretched out her arm, fingers just brushing the edge of the nest. The shiny thing glinted temptingly—it was smaller than she thought. With one last push she heaved herself up, grabbing a fistful of twigs and the prize within.

She let out a loud whoop of victory just as her foot slipped; she heard Jinho shout as she suddenly dropped, caught only by the ropes going painfully tight around her.

"G-got it!" she laughed, opening her hand to reveal a ring. It was a silver nearly as white as Chehang himself, carved with patterns she didn't recognize. Pretty. She slipped it onto her finger, heart still pounding from the rush of the fall.

"Sohmeng Par, don't you *ever*—" Jinho began, but then stopped, face going pale.

"Jinho, what—!"

She dropped then. Just slightly. Just enough for her gaze to follow Jinho's, up to where the rope had been shredded against the mountain. The fibres were snapping, strained by the force of her fall, unable to hold her body weight.

Jinho whistled sharply through his teeth, rapidly signaling up to Pasme Ker even as his voice stayed soft. "Sohmeng, just stay still, alright? Don't move, we're going to get you—we're going to get you back up."

"Jinho," she said, her mouth suddenly so dry, her words tangled in a gut-churning web. She saw the fraying rope, the viciously sharp cliffs above, Jinho's signals going too fast and too slow all at once. Numbly, she flexed her fingers against the mountain, feeling how little there was to hold on to, and she couldn't believe that her stupidity was actually going to be what killed her, that her first day out was going to end this way, that one careless glance from the gods was all it took to—

The rope snapped.

She was falling too quickly to take a breath, too suddenly to even scream—Jinho was screaming enough for them both, calling something that must have been her name. Desperate for something to grab onto, she reached for the cliff and tore through her palms like skinning a fruit. Each battering strike of the mountain's rogue branches sent her vision to sparking. Her shin clanged against the rocks as she kicked off, not wanting to be completely flayed before she hit the ground—oh godless night, the *ground*—

Eiji was getting closer. Bigger. Brighter. The air caught in Sohmeng's throat on the way to her lungs, stifling her cries. Death was so close, and she couldn't even find the air to argue.

She punched through the canopy, meeting wood and vine and leaves, slowing and stopping and tumbling once more in a terrible, infinite loop. By the time her back hit something solid, it was with a gentleness like being caught.

Mom? she thought, far from herself. *Dad?*

And then the world went quiet, and Sohmeng went quietly with it.

Part Two: Eiji

FIVE

WAKING WAS A SLOW and painful thing. Sohmeng attempted it several times, her eyes fluttering open just long enough for her body to shut down in response, unprepared for the reality it was being faced with. Her thoughts were hesitant to come together; when they did, they were mostly comprised of things like *godless night it hurts everywhere* and *I hope you're happy, you moron.*

"I'm not dead," she croaked.

The world around her didn't take much notice. She rasped in a breath, and a sharp elastic pain snapped deep in her right side. A broken rib? A branch through her torso? She didn't feel emotionally equipped to investigate at the moment.

"I'm not dead," she repeated, and the delirious laugh that heaved from her opened a whole new world of pain.

Yet, her mind chimed in usefully. *Not dead yet.*

Sohmeng closed her eyes, counting through the lunar phases: *Par, Go, Hiwei, Fua, Tang, Sol, Jão, Pel, Dongi, Se, Won,*

Nor, Chisong, Heng, Li, Ginhãe, Mi, Ker, Hiun, Ãofe, Soon, Nai, Tos, Jeji, Minhal. The irony was not lost on her that she was seeking solace in the gods that had finally thrown her from the mountainside for her audacity, sixteen years late.

First, she wiggled her fingers. Then her toes. Bit by bit, she woke her body back up to itself, taking note of the damage: a wrist either broken or sprained from grabbing at a tree branch, the carnage that was once her shin courtesy of the rocks, the panging in her ankle from where she'd kicked off Fochão Dangde. She loosened the harness at her hips, groaning with relief at the tingling sensation of returned bloodflow. Her belly chafed from where the rope had dug in.

It struck her that if she wasn't dying here on her back, these injuries were probably what had saved her. Assorted vegetation had broken her fall into a series of smaller falls—an agonizing lesson in protection from an indifferent drop.

But I think my clothes got ripped, she thought numbly. *Dad's going to be so—*

No. That wasn't right, was it?

Sohmeng took a long, slow breath in, trying to get the world around her to come back into focus. Rust-coloured vines wound around twisting tree trunks; enormous leaves glistened with dew in the light, shimmered like, like—what was it she had seen?

She raised her hand to her face, amber skin shaved down to scarlet. The silver ring on her finger glimmered cheerfully through smears of blood.

You idiot, she thought, clenching her fist. *You absolute idiot.*

She sucked in a breath through her teeth, braced herself, and turned her head both ways, letting out a sob of relief when nothing crunched. Slowly, she sat her body up, nauseous from the throbbing deep in her lower back. Her kidneys, maybe? She leaned against a tree trunk, tucking her knees to her chest with great effort, and gazed at the underworld she had fallen into.

Sohmeng hadn't landed on the valley floor proper, but rather upon one of the lower plateaus that sprawled down into the rest of the jungle. A lucky thing—had she ended up on one of the mountain's ledges, she'd have been forced to sit there and wait for whatever came sniffing for supper. Monkeys called to each other and insects rubbed their little legs in song, and mist slunk through the rustling leaves to lay moisture gently upon her like a blanket. There was comfort in the way the trees enveloped her, gave the illusion of being cocooned. More like being swaddled than suffocated. For a while she sat and observed, calm.

Until, of course, she wasn't.

Sohmeng's ribs burned as she vomited into the soil, the deadly reality of her situation sending her grappling like she was falling all over again—she needed to get out of here, she needed to *hide*, burning godseye, she was in the jungle by herself in the middle of sãoni territory and no one—

No one was coming for her.

None of the parties that went down ever made it back up. Not the warriors, or the volunteer explorers, or the miserable hãokar. Why would they send someone down for just one girl? Particularly a girl who had caused nothing but trouble? Sohmeng pulled herself to standing on legs of molten wax, grabbing onto rough tree bark to keep from falling, wincing as it split the cuts on her palms.

There was no way up; Ateng was so far away she couldn't even fathom a way to measure the distance. So down it was.

She made the trek the only way that she could: one shambling footfall after another, searching for any steadying branch that happened to reach out to her. Each step was precarious, alerting her to the bruises that moaned in their pre-life across her body, but also reassuring her that she was not, in fact, too broken to move. But was that a good thing? Surviving the fall was not necessarily a mercy, not when sãoni and poisonous plants and all manner of other dangers lay in the jungle. Her initial luck had only prolonged the inevitable.

And yet, against all reason, she was happy to be alive.

She pushed aside a heavy vine, marvelling at the leathery texture, and couldn't help but wonder in her delirium if her parents had once walked this way. In her youth, they had spent several phases a year gathering food from Eiji, trading with the other hmun in the network, keeping back the occasional wandering sãoni. After the Sky Bridge fell, they were among the first of the search parties to descend into the land the beasts had taken to swarming.

Had they made camp on this plateau? Had they sought answers from the languages of life all around, thrumming so wildly in the air? Had they also thought this place was beautiful before it consumed them?

Sohmeng stumbled and clutched a tree, spitting up mouthfuls of bile.

Come on, she thought, wiping her mouth with a shaking arm, *now is not the time for this kind of swooning. You can survive this. Live now. Panic later.*

After all, just because the search parties hadn't come back didn't mean that they were all dead. They were sent off with a mission to recover the trapped batengmun from Sodão Dangde and raise the Sky Bridge once again. For the warriors, it was an honour. For the hãokar, who had been exiled for crimes against the hmun, it was a chance at redemption. For the traders, it was just another adventure, this time with higher stakes.

People are resourceful, Sohmeng insisted to herself. *They could be alive even now. They could help me. The ancients survived the fall of the Last City of Polhmun Ão—this is nothing compared to the end of the world.*

Granted, those ancients had not been surrounded by the recent influx of sãoni, who were quick to devour every meaty thing in sight.

Sohmeng shook her head gently, trying to relieve the soft drone that had begun building in her ears. *No,* she reminded herself, *I said panic later. Right now, I'm figuring out how to stay alive.*

She licked her lips, shuddering at the foul taste of

apricots and stomach acid. That was it: water. Instead of panicking, she would find water, and she would drink it, and she would clean the blood from her leg and her hands and gods knew where else. There had to be a river around here somewhere; she had seen them from the mountain.

There. She smiled. No need to panic.

And then she heard it.

The sound could have been mistaken for the grinding of beetles' wings, or the rhythmic snapping of wood, easy to miss in the cacophony of a jungle teeming with life. Anyone else could have kept walking, ignorant of just how long they had been followed. But Lahni Par and Tonão Sol had not raised their children to be careless with their lives.

The feeling struck Sohmeng first in the gut. A prey instinct, activated. The hum of stony clicks suddenly sounded very close and very far at once, a sign that it was coming not from one being but many—the volume grew sickening, punctuated by the beating of wings and the screech of fleeing monkeys.

The roar that broke through the jungle was a sound Sohmeng had heard many times in her nightmares; she felt it like the tearing of a cuticle.

She looked around desperately, suddenly alert with primal fear. What did she have? Some rope, a basket full of smashed eggs, a ring she was apparently willing to die for. She gritted her teeth, grabbing a large stick off the ground, feeling stupid in advance for all the good it would do her.

The humming died down; the silence that came over the clearing was almost worse. It was torture, to anticipate her own death. Desperately, she tried to believe that perhaps nothing was there, that she had made up the danger in her own delirium.

Then they were upon her, and there was nothing left to deny.

The sāoni: like gargantuan salamanders slung low to the ground, their leathery skin night-dark and pebbled. Their flat faces were crowned with pointed head spines, and they had eyes like oracles, deep green and sour yellow, with pupils that were terrifying in their intelligence. The bright stripes along the sides of their thick necks led up to the main event: two rows of tiny, pointed, glistening teeth, competing in fright-factor only with the large sable claws that decorated all six of their powerful legs. Their tails flicked and whirled, hitting the ground with heavy thumps.

Sohmeng Par had hoped never to see a sāoni up close in her life. It had been bad enough from far away, when the Bridge fell; the predators' calls, the weeping of the hmun backed into the caves, the sick snap of rope as everyone on the Bridge was lost. She clutched her stick uselessly, stumbling backward as more and more eyes blinked open in the jungle. So many of them, silent until they chose not to be.

The largest of the sāoni stepped forward so suddenly that she cried out on instinct. The beast tilted its head, exposing a bumpy neck with purple stripes, before making a noise back at her, flicking its blue tongue between its teeth. Sohmeng's back hit a tree. Was it mocking her?

From behind the large sãoni came another, smaller and quicker, with bright green throat stripes. It nudged the large one with a series of chattering clicks and growls, tapping its claws as it stared hungrily at Sohmeng. Without thinking, she reached for her basket, tossing it at them, wondering if she could distract them long enough to run. The smaller sãoni took notice, leaping upon the basket and devouring it whole. The crunch of the weaving made her feel sick.

If only she had the silvertongue plant, like the warriors carried. If only she had fallen while on guard duty, equipped to protect herself. If only she hadn't fallen at all. If only she hadn't been so much trouble. If only she had been nice to her brother, helpful to her grandmother, deserving of her parents.

If only her name were actually Sohmeng Par.

So many ifs, and none of them able to save her. The small sãoni was finished with the eggs and hungry for more. Sohmeng raised her weapon in shaking stinging hands and yelled, imprinting her furious indignance on the world around her with all she had left—and the sãoni was encroaching and the growling and shrieking got louder and despite her best efforts to go with grace, all she could think was—

Godless or not, no one deserves to die like this.

Six

THEN THERE CAME another sound.

It was different from the rest, a growl sized for a smaller throat. The sãoni were undeterred—the smaller green-striped one crouched low, pulling its shoulders back in preparation to leap. Sohmeng braced herself for impact, but the sound cut through the forest again: a shriek, a howl.

The creature it came from bounded fearlessly toward the sãoni, vaulting over the largest one's head and landing in front of it with another splitting cry. It was human sized and shaped, but its body was covered in scales, and its claws—

Wait, no—she blinked, realizing what she was seeing: a human being, clothed in sãoni skin, yelling with all the fury of a newborn child.

The large sãoni yielded, bowing its head to peer at the defiant creature that stood before it. The smaller sãoni snuck to the side, ready to lunge at Sohmeng, but the human intervened, their voice storm-wild; the animal screamed back, and the human matched it once more, stretching their body to a strange contortion that made them appear larger.

Sensing an opportunity, Sohmeng stepped back—but the pack took notice, rumbling warnings in eerie unison. The human turned and glared at her with eyes that very nearly matched those of the sãoni; their expression stopped Sohmeng in her tracks, leaving her uncharacteristically speechless.

The human hissed, glancing between the mean-looking sãoni with the green stripes and Sohmeng. They clenched their fists, the claws hooked over their fingers curling and uncurling in graceful indecision. And then they turned to Sohmeng with an arch in their back that made her feel horribly hunted.

"I, I'm not—" she started, but the human silenced her with a series of low, menacing clicks. Sohmeng gripped her stick, ready to strike, but then the human—

Started . . . dancing?

At least, that was her best guess. They leapt around Sohmeng in a series of dramatic gestures, making impossible-sounding noises. They hopped and crouched and crawled, and the whole time the sãoni watched in perfect stillness, making no move to encroach further on Sohmeng. Which was more than fine with her.

That is, until the human rushed in and bit her hard on the neck.

"AIE—" she shouted, swatting at them, but they had

already yanked back, grimacing. "What under the godseye was THAT?"

"Me saving your life," the human snapped, roughly pushing back a tooth-lined hood to reveal their face in full.

The striking green of their eyes was emphasized by charcoal makeup that had been smeared from their eyebrows to their sharp cheekbones. Their hair was nearly as dark as Sohmeng's, but hacked artlessly short. Though they weren't much taller than she was, their glowering presence made Sohmeng feel like she was being loomed over.

"You BIT me," Sohmeng squeaked.

"I had to!" They grumbled out a few more nonsensical noises. Sohmeng opened her mouth to start yelling, as was her right, but they shut her down with another glare. "It's part of the—the courtship ritual. I marked you as a mate so the colony wouldn't eat you. You're welcome."

And just like that they turned on their heel, stalking furiously toward the sāoni, who had become surprisingly docile. The purple one batted at them with one of its mid legs, but rather than drop to the ground in terror like any reasonable human would do, they shoved off the touch, growling in what sounded like exasperation. The sāoni chirped, and the others echoed it.

"Sorry, no, what?" Sohmeng stumbled forward, hesitating as she passed the creatures that were now peering at her innocently—the same creatures that had been hunting her five minutes ago. She swallowed her fear, letting herself be carried by adrenaline alone. "No, I think I need more of an explanation than that."

"What you need is clear rainwater and some spiceroot before you turn into a walking infection. And seeing as you're now my problem, I would appreciate it if you cooperated."

"Your *problem*?" Sohmeng was feeling a lot of different ways, and none of them were cooperative. "I don't even know what just happened. Those things were stalking me, and then you popped out and screamed at them and you *bit* me—"

"I already told you, I did it to save your life!" the human retorted, shoving at an enormous sãoni tail that kept trying to curl around their waist. "You know, it wasn't great for me either. I don't even *know* you, that's not how I wanted to—ugh. Just . . . come here. Mama can carry you, you're in no condition to even be standing."

"*Mama?*"

The human let out a high click, nodding to the large purple sãoni with the ridged throat. It flattened its head to the ground, seemingly in response. Sohmeng stared in wonder, all of her instincts reduced to so much babbling noise. Or maybe it was just the bloodloss. Or the shock— she was probably totally in shock.

"Who are you?" she asked. Her options for survival may have been limited, but that didn't mean she was about to follow this freak completely in the dark.

"Just hook your leg here. Mind her cheeks."

"No, but who—" Sohmeng stumbled on her bad ankle.

Before she knew it, the sãoni's—Mama's—snout was nudging her. She flailed back, and the human hissed in frustration, taking her roughly into their arms. The pressure on her side made her yelp. Mama rumbled, pupils narrowing on the human; in response they chirped, looking uncertainly at Sohmeng before pressing their grimy cheek to hers.

Nope. No way. "If you bite me again," she muttered, squirming away to the best of her ability, "I swear on both the gods *and* my grandmother—"

The human ignored this, hoisting Sohmeng up between Mama's fore- and mid legs. They settled in behind her, their strong arms firm around her waist as they grasped the sãoni's neck. Then the pack was moving, faster than Sohmeng's body was ready for. She scrunched her eyes shut, willing herself not to be sick again.

Several sharp somethings dug into Sohmeng's back—the small sãoni teeth that were sewed onto the human's hood. Despite herself, she slumped against them. "Can I at least have your name? I'm Sohmeng Par, by the way. Thanks for asking."

The human uttered another chirp, this time followed by three clicks; the sãoni repeated it among themselves, a strange chorus barrelling through the woods.

"Great trick," mumbled Sohmeng, "but seeing as you're apparently my *mate* and all, I figure I deserve to know—"

"That was it," said the human, humour and annoyance tinging their words in equal measure.

"Okay. Let me rephrase. Give me a name I can actually

pronounce. One that might give me any idea as to what sort of mate I am apparently the proud new owner of." After all, without a phasal association or any introductory pronouns, Sohmeng had no idea where to even start gendering this stranger beyond the respectful neutral. *What an absurd problem*, she thought distantly. What a ridiculous thing to worry about after the day she'd had.

The lull stretched between them long enough that Sohmeng was confident she wasn't going to get an answer. She turned her attention instead to the verdant jungle, with its slim saplings poking boldly out of the understory, dwarfed by leaves as large as her whole torso. A great web of vines stretched out high above, reaching farther than she could see. The colony travelled at a solid pace, crossing over bubbling creeks and weaving around enormous trees, their great claws crunching the detritus of the forest floor. Eventually, the movement lulled Sohmeng enough that her eyes drifted shut.

"Hei," the human said, stirring her from her rest.

"Mm?"

"My name. Hei. Call me Hei."

It was almost nothing to work with. No hint of phase or gender in sight. But Sohmeng could say it, and that was a start. "Fine," she mumbled, "Hei." With a single question answered, her mind's racing slowed to a shamble, and she allowed her body to relax as much as it could atop the roaming body of Ateng's greatest enemy.

Seven

CALL IT NAÏVE, but Sohmeng had sort of expected healing to feel better than getting bashed up in the first place.

"Godless *night* that burns—!" she hissed.

Her wounds had been cleaned out with a mix of boiled rainwater and the sharply-scented juice of a small green fruit. It had stung fiercely, prompting her to swat at Hei more than once. Now, the world's chompiest healer was rubbing a mess of mashed up herbs into the wounds while Sohmeng nearly jumped out of what little skin she had left.

"Godless, moonless, loveless *hãokar*, are your hands made of *rubble*—"

Hei made a little noise, a tapping at the back of their throat, and reached for a swath of what appeared to be sãoni skin, saved in a bag they kept strapped to one of Mama's head spines. Since they rode off together on the creature's back, Hei had been subdued, only breaking the silence with their peculiar clicking—talking?—with the sãoni.

On Sohmeng's part, anxiety and agitation had been the two ruling feelings of the day, oscillating back and forth faster than she could keep up with. From what she could glean, Hei didn't seem to be any more at ease. Unsurprising; they probably hadn't started their day expecting to find the twitching remains of a loud-mouthed idiot in the middle of their jungle. She knew she ought to be more grateful to the person who had just saved her life, but frankly, Hei was weird. Hei was unpredictable. Hei clicked like a reptile and bumped noses with sãoni.

It was kind of a lot to take in.

One of the sãoni huffed, thumping its back leg against a thick tree trunk. What Sohmeng had thought were falling leaves fluttered up again, revealing themselves to be butterflies, moving in a rainbow of synchronization across the canopy. *For a complete death sentence,* Sohmeng thought, *the jungle's got a pretty nice view.*

Hei made a soft, birdlike coo, reaching for Mama. Sohmeng stared in shock as her saviour stuck their entire arm into Mama's big, bumpy cheek. They pulled it out, still in one piece and slick with saliva.

"What are you—oh *seriously*?" Sohmeng whined in protest as Hei wiped it on top of the herb mash they had applied.

Hei shushed her, wrapping her leg in a swath of sãoni skin. "It's good for you. It will harden as it dries. Seal the wound to keep out sickness."

"It's *spit*."

"You bled on her. Only fair she spits on you." Hei trilled

at Mama, who puffed air through her nostrils in a way Sohmeng took to be laughter.

"It's disgusting," she muttered, not quite brave enough to argue any further. She sighed heavily, watching Hei tie off their makeshift bandages. While everything else on their person seemed to come from Eiji, a mishmash of survivalist ingenuity, their bag had the distinct style of Ateng's crafts-manship, complete with faded patterns of the twenty-five lunar phases. "How did you learn all this?"

"Practice." Hei shrugged. "Luck."

"Did you have a teacher?" she asked. Hei nodded to the sãoni without a trace of irony, tying the bag back onto Mama's head spines. "...like, any *people* though?" Hei made a sound Sohmeng couldn't even begin to interpret. This was getting ridiculous. "Bear with me, because this might come as a shock, but I am a *human person* that does not speak—I don't know, *Sãonipa*."

"Maybe you should learn," Hei said, turning to pat Mama's cheeks. "After all, you're in their—" They noticed Sohmeng poking at her bandages and whistled sharply, fixing their green eyes on her with disapproval. Sohmeng jumped, scowling as a couple of the sãoni peered at Hei in response to the apparent reprimand.

"Is it really so difficult to answer a few questions?" Sohmeng continued messing with the bandages, deter-mined to keep Hei's attention on her long enough to get a response. She was well-practiced in the art of being difficult to ignore. "I'm not asking for your most intim-ate secrets—just the basic things! Who are you? How do I gender you? Why aren't you up in the hmun?" Hei hissed irritably through their teeth, grimacing. Sohmeng took the reaction as a sign to keep pushing. "I mean, you *are* from Ateng, right? Your voice, it's not shaped like a trader's—the accent's different in the vowels." She remembered hearing it in her parents' voices as they practiced Dulpongpa over the fire, the small differences distinct as veins of woven-stone. She cleared her throat. "I don't even know what the other hmuns' dialects would be like, so—you sound like me. Like one of us."

"One of you."

Their tone was like the yanking of a cord: tight and abrupt and full of potential energy. Looking at Hei, with their tooth-ornamented hood and the cautious hunch of their shoulders, their choppy hair and the charcoal rubbed thick around their eyes, Sohmeng could see how foolish she must have sounded. "I just mean—"

"I only speak Hmunpa for you, Sohmeng Par." Once more, the words were sharp, made doubly so by Hei's piercing eye contact. Apparently even falling from Ateng wasn't enough to keep Sohmeng from hearing her name as an insult.

"What?" she challenged, refusing to back down. "You'd prefer to shriek and growl and act like an animal?"

"I *am* an animal," Hei said, stepping toward her with a fierce look, and Sohmeng flinched despite herself, aware of the state of her body and how unevenly matched they were. Seeing this, Hei moved no further, even as their voice stayed shale-sharp. "And so are you. So are we all.

It would serve you to remember that, now that you're down from your ever-wise hmun."

Sohmeng was well-aware that this was the perfect time for her survival instinct to step in, pat her on the shoulder, and encourage her to take a seat. But as always, her curiosity belayed that order, drawing her attention to the human standing terribly close to her, their hurt nearly tangible.

She considered their extensive knowledge of the jungle, their disdain for speaking like a human being, their choice to save the life of someone they could barely tolerate, their lunar cycle bag in tatters, their snarling contempt for the hmun.

"You're hãokar, aren't you?" Sohmeng asked, unable to help herself.

She prepared for an explosive reaction, a sãoni shriek or a hard shove. Wasn't that to be expected of an exile? But Hei did nothing of the sort; their shoulders dropped slightly from their defensive stance, and for a long moment they were quiet, brow furrowed as they stared at nothing in particular.

"Hãokar," they echoed at last, looking up at Sohmeng with a softness that ached, an expression that might have been relief. "I suppose I am."

And at that, even Sohmeng had to fall silent.

As the day progressed, the jungle filled in the gap between them: the rising and falling hum of insects, the playful song of the frogs who would feast upon them. The sãoni were constantly growling or chirping, social as the monkeys that swung enthusiastically across the canopy. Even though they weren't speaking to Sohmeng, Hei still made plenty of noise, interacting with the sãoni with ease. A drastic difference from the high-strung, awkward person who communicated with Sohmeng primarily in grunts and cagey looks.

Viunwei would say that's how any reasonable person would treat her. Her fists clenched at the thought, stinging the scrapes on her hands through the paste Hei had cooked up. What would her brother be thinking right now? For all he knew, she was dead, crunched at the bottom of the rainforest like a beetle underfoot. And Jinho—he was probably blaming himself, even though it was her own stupid fault. If, by some miracle, she ever made it back up to the hmun, she had a lot to apologize for.

She examined the silver ring wrapped snugly around her middle finger. In the light, it glinted with a brightness reminiscent of the stripes of the sãoni-repelling silvertongue plant. She thought about waving her hand just to see if it would ward them off, if it would shake the surface of her vision and prove that this had been a dream all along.

Unlikely, if her throbbing wrist had anything to say about it.

A whistle broke across the clearing; Hei had their hood back up and claws on, and was standing in front of a group of tiny sãoni with their back arched, scuttling around like a spider that had tumbled into a fermenting barrel. The sãoni they were taunting, which Sohmeng guessed were babies, took the bait, leaping forward and wrestling with Hei. Sohmeng straightened up in alarm, watching for blood, but Hei only laughed as they wiggled their arm, wrapped in sãoni skin, from the creatures' mouths.

She flexed her foot, feeling the tug of the raw skin beneath her own wrappings. The thick sheen of saliva Hei had smeared on was working, hardening into an elastic casing that reduced the itching pain of the injury. Much as she hated to admit it, their knowledge of the sãoni was proving itself to be sound. No, not knowledge—*familiarity*. There was a difference between studying sãoni from afar and literally playing between their jaws.

It raised a few concerns.

How had they come to join this colony? Were they completely delusional? What crime had they committed to get exiled? Had she known them before? Were there other hãokar like them, roaming the jungle and befriending the local predators?

"Sohmeng Par?"

She looked up, startled by Hei's voice. They had shaken off the tiny lizards and walked over to her while she was lost in thought, breathing hard from the exertion of sãoni wrestling.

"Hei the Elusive?" she replied, disappointed to hear that her exhaustion ruined the effect of the recalcitrance she was aiming for.

Hei rolled their eyes, pulling back their hood and crouching down to eye level with Sohmeng. She scanned their face for anger, for hostility left over from earlier, but instead was greeted with a surprising amount of civility. Perhaps even warmth. She held her arm closer to herself as the pause dragged on between them for a beat too long.

"...you're making a joke," Hei said at last, nodding somberly.

"Not a very good one if it takes you till next Par to get it," she said, a tense laugh escaping her lips.

"I'm not very funny," they replied. Sohmeng was trying to figure out the least insulting way to agree with that when Hei whistled through their front teeth, nodding their head at her. Sohmeng stared at them, uncomprehending, until Hei made the gesture again, this time waving at her arm. Without thinking, she held it out, making a face as her wristbones creaked.

Hei took her arm, turning it over in their hands with care. They tested her range of motion, humming sympathetically in response to her pained wincing. Behind them, Mama rested her great broad throat on the cool forest floor, watching closely.

"I realize that I haven't yet asked how you came to be hurt," they said as they bent back her fingers. "Forgive me. I was ... surprised. To see you." They leaned toward her, brushing their filthy cheek against hers. Sohmeng tried not to cringe; she didn't want to be rude again, particularly in the face of such jarring sincerity.

"I sort of ... fell."

"From one of the trees?"

"Technically, I guess, if you count all the shrubs I slammed into on the way down the cliffside," Sohmeng mused, her back aching in response to the attempted humour about her own near-death experience.

Hei's eyes went wide with disbelief. "You fell from the *mountain?*"

Sohmeng nodded. "Off the side of it. Like a rock, straight down. Well, no, I might have spun around a few times while I was scrabbling for some godless thing to grab onto. It's kind of a blur."

Hei turned to Sohmeng's shredded hands, their face still lemur-like with surprise. Up close, they looked a lot more human than they probably cared to be told—strong square jaw, honest, expressive eyes, a freckle that interrupted the slope of their upper lip. Beneath the sãoni skin, their body was stocky, muscular, with broad shoulders and gently curved hips. For an exiled lunatic with a disastrous haircut, Sohmeng mused, they were pretty handsome.

She cleared her throat, daintily wiggling her fingers. "Got a cool ring out of it, though. Stole it from a bird. Talk about divine retribution, huh?"

Hei glanced at the silver band, frowning slightly. "It's a miracle you survived," they murmured, circling Sohmeng with newfound concern, animal in their motions as they inspected her, turning her neck one way and the other.

"Well if you pull my head off—"

"Why would I do that?"

"To eat it, maybe. You run with a crowd that's pretty notorious for biting heads off."

Hei blew an annoyed exhale through their nose, releasing their hands from the base of Sohmeng's skull and turning back to face her. "That's not—it's a misconception."

Sohmeng laughed loudly, forcing her heart rate steady as a whole mess of images and memories tangled up in her mind. "Oh *really*—"

"Yes!" Hei insisted as they dropped into a crouch. "Really. It's true that sãoni can and will eat humans, and some colonies will target them in specific circumstances, but generally, humans aren't their preferred prey. Most of the time, they're just reacting to a territory conflict, or—"

"Actually," Sohmeng said, crossing her arms with a tense smile, "I changed my mind. I'd rather not discuss the dietary preferences of the monsters that have been picking off my hmun for the past three years."

"They aren't monsters," Hei snapped. "And Mama has nothing to do with that. Fochão Dangde isn't even my family's territory!"

"Your *family*—" Sohmeng began, voice rising in anger, but was interrupted by a long, loud growl from Mama. The sãoni reached out a front leg, swatting in their direction. Sohmeng balked, and Hei backed off sheepishly. Regardless of whether Sohmeng understood Sãonipa, she recognized a scolding when she saw one. How many times had her grandmother sent Sohmeng and Viunwei off to do separate tasks after a squabble? How many times had her mother hushed her with a single look?

She leaned her head back, following the pattern of the vines above to try and slow her racing thoughts. While the sãoni had not devoured her just yet, she could not escape her history and the part these creatures played in it. She was making a point of trying to appear fearless, but there was more trepidation inside of her than she cared to admit. She glanced at Hei—Hei, who had shared and lost the same hmun as Sohmeng. Hei the exile. Hãokar.

Sohmeng thought of Grandmother Mi patiently reminding her of the different worlds everyone lived in: her brother Viunwei Soon in his world of responsibility, young Tanshi Ginhãe the oracle in her world of conflicting futures, batty old Esteona Nor, getting lost in the caves and singing in a world where her family had not been cursed with Minhal. A world for each of her neighbours, and all of them unknowable.

Sohmeng glared up at a bright fungus growing from a tree, feeling sufficiently chastised. She had known Hei for less than a day—it was impossible to understand a thing about their world, and unfair to snap because her own had unexpectedly changed. She glanced over at Mama, who watched them with narrowed eyes, cheeks puffed and bumpy. Idly, she noticed that the sãoni's purple throat stripes had begun to glow softly as the sun went down.

Hoping that she wasn't about to make an idiot of herself, Sohmeng leaned in and pressed her cheek to Hei's.

They started, their shoulders lowering uncertainly from their ears. She took it as a small victory.

"So where *is* your family's territory?" she asked, picking up a fallen stick and poking at the ground. Behind them,

Mama closed her eyes and laid down, tucking her forelegs neatly underneath her.

"Where they roam," Hei replied, their voice as careful as Sohmeng's. Navigating around each other's personalities seemed to be a struggle on both ends. "Sãoni migrate throughout the seasons. Or, they try to. But the route's been … disrupted." Their eyes turned dark as they fidgeted with the claws on their fingers.

"Disrupted?"

"Hmun are stepping out of their bounds. It's gotten in the way of the sãoni migration route, pushing colonies to where they can't thrive. Many of them are stagnating, becoming territorial. The colony on Fochão Dangde is a pretty good example of that—I can't remember the last time they moved as they're supposed to. You're lucky it was us who found you. That colony has a taste for—" They caught themself. "They're less compassionate, toward humans."

"Yeah," Sohmeng said, not meeting their eye. "I've gathered that."

"My family—we're still migrating. For now." Hei leaned back against a tree trunk, gently pushing aside the fronds of a fern that tickled their forehead. "It looks like we're on our way to the Ãotul River. We'll follow its path north, I imagine. Do what we can to avoid any of the other territorial colonies."

Sohmeng's heart squeezed at the mention of the Ãotul—it had glittered like a gem in the view from Ateng. She could only imagine what it would look like up close.

But that wasn't what she should be focusing on right now. "Is it really that big a deal if we bump into another colony?" she asked, gesturing to the sãoni pawing at trees, curling up in heaps of heavy tails and glowing throats. It was remarkable, how benign they could look. "They're all sãoni, aren't they?"

"Being of the same species is not the same as being allies." Hei laughed softly to themself—it was not a happy sound. "Sãoni don't tend to bond outside of their own colonies. They don't trade like humans, and they don't compromise on their leadership. Too many of them in one place is a recipe for bloodshed—it's why they used to keep a healthy distance from one another on the migration route. But a stable colony is secure, like my family."

The babies were climbing along the mean-looking sãoni with the green-striped throat, squeaking and biting at its head spines. Occasionally it would nudge them off, but for the most part it tolerated their antics, wriggling into the earth in search of a comfortable spot to sleep.

"For the most part, we avoid Fochão Dangde and the trouble that would come with it. Their alpha is older, more mellow. All she seeks is food. If we keep our distance, there's no trouble." The statement would have been reassuring to Sohmeng, if the food in question wasn't human flesh. She swallowed, watching the babies play, unsure of how to respond. "We have more trouble with Sodão Dangde. Their alpha is difficult."

"Difficult how?"

"She and Mama..." Hei frowned. "Ownership of the

mountain is a point of contention between them. They used to be in a stagnant colony there together, before Mama went her separate way. Now it belongs to . . ." They searched for a name to give to the alpha. "To Blacktooth. If Mama gets too close, it's mayhem. They just provoke each other, I can't really explain it."

"Have you tried asking her?" Sohmeng asked dryly. *"Hello Mother, a growling biting morning to you, why can't we go climb that nice mountain all together?"*

"That's not how their language works," Hei said, narrowing their eyes at her suspiciously, "and I have a feeling you know it."

"I only know what I'm told." Sohmeng grinned in spite of herself, leaning back on her arms—which would have been fine if it weren't for the whole broken wrist issue. She squawked, yanking her arm back to her chest and hissing curses.

Hei jumped up, going to her side and examining the injury. "We really ought to get spiceroot for that. It'll dull the pain, bring the swelling down. The taste isn't so bad, either."

"Incredible," said Sohmeng. "Can we grate it over dinner or what? How spicy is it? I'm not trying to burn my tongue off, here."

"You'll have to wait to find out. We have to harvest it first." Sohmeng's shoulders slumped. Nothing could ever be that easy, could it? She was about to bemoan the complete unfairness of the situation, but was paused by the grim look on Hei's face.

"What?" she asked warily, already dreading the answer.

"That rival territory I just mentioned? That's the closest place I've seen it grow, and the easiest to get to by half."

That meant Sodão Dangde. Sohmeng swallowed, uncomfortable showing this stranger how complicated she felt about heading toward what was once her second home—for reasons beyond bloodthirsty sãoni. "There's seriously *nothing* else I can chew on that'll fix it?" she groaned.

"Nothing that will work as well." They ran a hand through their mop of hair, sighing. "If we keep at this pace, we should be close enough to spot some spiceroot in a few days' time. We're fortunate that it grows en route to the Ãotul, even if it does bring us closer to Blacktooth than I'd like."

"Right," Sohmeng muttered, deflating. "Lucky us."

The babies' squeaking got louder, prompting an annoyed rumble from the sleepy, green-throated sãoni. With a condoling click Sohmeng's way, Hei went to intervene; Sohmeng was left to consider precisely which spices to baste herself with in the time she had left. After all, no one in the world was fortunate enough to avoid becoming a meal for the sãoni twice in a week.

EIGHT

"EEEE—RKK?"

"Not quite. More lift in the first sound."

"YeeARCK?"

"No, you don't really voice the second part. It's in the back of your throat. More like this." Seated behind Sohmeng, Hei let out a sound like grinding gravel, loud enough to get the attention of all the sāoni. Realizing what they'd done, Hei released a few clicks of apology, earning a string of irritated growls and a swat from Mama's tail for the false alarm they had raised. They cleared their throat with a sheepish smile. "Does that make more sense?"

"I have no idea how you remember all of this," Sohmeng said, rubbing the ear Hei had screeched into. They nudged it with their nose, and Sohmeng tried not to pull back.

Three days of close proximity had yet to help Sohmeng get over the amount of physical affection Hei tended to display. From what she could see, a lack of regard for personal space was a trait consistent among most of the sãoni. But they were animals—it was far more bizarre to have another human be so open with their body, particularly when they weren't exactly the talkative type. Hei nursed her injuries with familial care, and had taken to detangling Sohmeng's hair with their fingers, as though their relationship was one of intimacy and not mere tolerance. When the two of them rattled each other's nerves enough that Mama took notice, Hei was always quick to press cheeks.

Odd as it was, Sohmeng couldn't really complain about the dynamic that was currently keeping her alive. Hei had stabilized her wrist with a splint of tree bark and more sãoni skin, which had reduced its insistent twinging to something bearable. They gathered useful herbs as they could, and Mama's saliva was sealing up the scrapes on Sohmeng's hands quicker than she would have guessed. The pains in her body had fully established themselves, giving Sohmeng a better idea of which injuries were minor and which were more severe. While she was eager to get to the spiceroot so she might actually sleep through a night, she had to admit that she was grateful for the recovery time their journey imposed.

"How much longer now, do you think?" she asked, stroking tentatively between Mama's head spines and earning a pleased rumble. Beside her, the vicious green-throated sãoni that she had come to call Green Bites let out a squawk, wanting a pat as well, which Sohmeng did not indulge; she'd nearly been chomped last time. Hei said he was just *at that age*, fickle and temperamental, but Sohmeng wasn't so quick to forgive.

"We should be able to find some spiceroot by tomorrow, I hope," said Hei. The colony's movement through the forest was mostly dependent on Mama, whose whims were not always easy to track. Sohmeng was baffled that Hei's wants had any influence at all, but Hei was baffling in general. "I've been keeping an eye out for the flower, just in case any strays are growing this far out. Is your wrist hurting again?"

"No more than the rest of me." The sãoni meandered into a clearing, a spot where the dense treetops opened up to reveal Sodão Dangde watching proudly over the valley, closer than Sohmeng realized. By the moons, these lizards moved quickly. She absently slid her hands along Mama's cheeks, prompting a deeper growl out of the sãoni.

"I hope that's a good sound," Sohmeng said, laughing nervously.

"It is," Hei replied fondly. "She likes you." They took Sohmeng's good hand, guiding it along the sãoni's cool, leathery skin. Mama's cheeks were bumpy on the outside, ridged in a way that most of the other sãoni were not.

"Why do her cheeks look funny?" she asked.

"She's holding her eggs," Hei said, sounding surprised that she didn't know. It was an annoying habit they had, assuming Sohmeng hadn't spent all of her life in a literal cave and just knew these sorts of things. "Her saliva has hardening properties to keep them from cracking prematurely."

"She holds them in her *mouth?*" Sohmeng asked, horrified.

"The pockets in her cheeks," they clarified, reaching around to smooth the outline of one of Mama's eggs, smiling. The sãoni responded with a chirp and three clicks. A couple of the others looked back in their direction again as they scuttled along, echoing their alpha.

"What did she say?"

"My name." Hei repeated the sound, an aura of tenderness coming over them.

Out of Hei's mouth, the sound was more familiar—they had made it after they rescued her, hadn't they? But it was surprising to hear it from the sãoni. Sohmeng had made up little Hmunpa names for the reptiles, but she hadn't imagined they would have naming systems of their own. To be fair, she hadn't thought of them as much more than killers before she landed in Eiji. "How do you know that's what they're saying?"

"They direct it at me. And the context makes sense, it's two sounds, two words, together—hatchling and food."

"They call you Baby Dinner?"

Hei bristled at that, stuttering an unintelligible reply from behind her. Sohmeng's self-satisfied snickering was promptly cut off by Hei's choice to lean down and bite her sharply on the shoulder. She yelled, reaching back to swat at Hei, who easily blocked the blow by grabbing her arm.

"You," they said, ducking away from a swing from Sohmeng's bad wrist, "are very rude."

"So I've been told," she snorted. "Every day of my life."

"By who?" asked Hei, suddenly sounding very ready to defend Sohmeng's honour.

"You sure are invested for the person who called me rude in the first place!" Sohmeng laughed.

"Well you're my m—" They stopped abruptly, mumbling for a moment before letting out an agitated growl. "I just want to know who said this thing."

"My brother, mostly. And don't take that tone, it's not like he's wrong. I'm pretty much the rudest person I know."

"Your brother?"

Speaking Viunwei's name felt a little like a summoning, and all at once Sohmeng's stomach clenched. She had been trying not to think too much about him or Grandmother Mi since she fell, particularly given the likelihood that they would never see each other again. Feeling the weight of his worry pressing on her back all the way from Fochão Dangde, she kept her eyes instead on Sodão Dangde—another set of siblings with an impossible gap between them.

Up on the mountain, she swore she saw something move, creeping along the edges of the cliffside. Some animal, or else some old ghost. There were so many ghosts in Ateng, so much wishful thinking.

"Yeah," she said, attempting nonchalance. "Yeah. Viunwei Soon. He's older than me. He looked after me after our—our parents died, and our grandmother took her Grand Ones' Vows. He's a real piece of work."

"He says you are rude?"

"Rude, loud, difficult, ungrateful—you name it. Being disappointed in me is pretty much his only hobby." Insulting him came easy to her. The normalcy of it was almost comforting. "We were close as kids, always playing and arguing. But in a good way, you know? And then he had his Tengmunji and came back as this … this totally different person. Serious all the time and worried about everything, like he had to be responsible for everyone. Even my parents could see it, but my mom said that it's normal for people to change after their Tengmunji, that I'd understand when my time came. Too bad I'll never know."

"You're a tengmun kar," Hei said, their voice gone soft with realization.

"Is it that obvious?" muttered Sohmeng, an old, angry instinct rising up within her.

"No, it's just—" They adjusted their grip on Mama. "No one else could be initiated, could they? After the Bridge fell."

Sohmeng nodded, fidgeting with the splint around her wrist. "Not with the rest of the hmun there, no." The unfairness of it railed within her as she played through the injustices that came with it: the denied entry into meaningful work, the ban on exploring adult relationships, the way she was talked down to despite all she did within the hmun. "Maybe that's why Viunwei's been so foul. Because he feels like he has to take care of me. I don't know."

Hei said nothing, reaching to play with Sohmeng's hair. She waited for them to break the silence, to dig into all the ways she was overreacting, to offer Prince Viunwei's perspective like she hadn't heard it all her life. But they kept quiet, offering only soothing touch and more space than Sohmeng knew she was allowed.

Despite the anxiety that tugged within her, she took the opportunity.

"Maybe—maybe things would be different if Mom and Dad were still here. They were good parents. They hunted outside Ateng and traded with other hmun in the network. When they'd come back, they always had all of these stories to tell, and it made me so proud that they were my parents, you know? Other kids' parents did boring, everyday things, but mine were explorers." Her mother used to spin her around after so many phases away; her father would bring home pressed flowers to introduce her to Eiji. Lahni Par and Tonão Sol. It was hard not to love them. Especially now that they were gone. "You know, even my damwei was pretty cool—he was a record keeper, he knew all of the stories. He could name every Fua back ten generations." Her heart squeezed with fondness at the memory. While some badamwei had little to do with the children they helped produce for the hmun, Rikelho had always been happy to spend time with her and Viunwei. They called him *Damdão Kelho*, and considered him a third parent. "He went down with the Bridge. A couple months later, my parents descended for an excursion to repair it. They never came back up. Same as everyone else who tried."

"I'm sorry," said Hei, and the sincerity in their voice

drew Sohmeng's attention to the heaviness that had closed around them thick as fog.

"Me too," she replied a little too hastily, uncertain of what she was apologizing for. Oversharing? Being a burden? Surviving the fall? But she wasn't sorry about any of those things. She wanted to survive, and to be honest, and if that meant causing trouble, she could live with it.

And so, it seemed, could Hei. Sohmeng picked at a thread on her tattered pants, knowing then what needed to be said. "Look, Hei, I know that after you saved me I was ... sort of touchy. Which wasn't fair, considering what you'd done for me. Like, yes, I had just fallen off a mountain and was feeling pretty lousy, but ..."

"You don't have to apologize," Hei said. The teeth on their hood pressed lightly into Sohmeng's back as they leaned in; she found she didn't mind. "It's understandable. I guess living out here I just ... I forgot. I forget, sometimes, how others might feel. I should have been more considerate."

As Sohmeng was trying to figure out how to reply to this unexpected reasonability, Mama lifted her head and released a bone-shaking bellow. Sohmeng squinted against the rays of the setting sun shining through the trees; evening was falling faster than she had noticed. She cleared her throat, taking a deep breath and trying to shake off the loss that still clung to her thorn-stubborn. "Bedtime?"

"It seems so." Sure enough, as they came to a clearing, the sāoni began the great quest for the coziest spot, climbing and piling, nipping and chirping. Hei held Sohmeng steady as Mama circled a few times until she slumped down in front of a large tree. "I can make a shelter for when the rain comes, and a fire. Roast a jackfruit, if you'd like something warm."

"Warm sounds nice." At the mention of food, Sohmeng's stomach rumbled. Even though she had hardly done any walking today, having stayed firmly put on Mama's back, the simple act of staying alive was taking up most of her energy. She was grateful when Hei helped her down. Together they sought out their own spot, one where they were less likely to have a sãoni roll over and squash them in the night.

Sohmeng leaned back against a mossy rock, watching the creatures pile atop each other, their throat stripes glowing as they prepared to rest. For deadly hunters, she had thought the sãoni would be light sleepers, or perhaps not even to sleep at all. Instead, she had learned that they became sluggish once the sun set and their body temperatures dropped with it.

In the midst of the sãoni heap, the babies—or *hatchlings* as Hei called them—climbed all over their mother, who huffed at them in annoyance. Hei gathered sticks to sharpen and spear into the ground, patting Mama's head fondly as they walked by. With a tightness in her throat, Sohmeng realized that this was closest thing to a family she had seen in a very long time.

A soft melancholy descended, leaving her unusually reserved for the rest of the evening. She kept her knees tucked to her chest, her injured arm pressed close to her heart, as if she could fold herself away from the rawness that had been opened up. Beside her, Hei kindled a fire with the dry vines hanging above and cooked their meal in companionable silence. After they had eaten, she stared up at the snippets of night sky visible through the canopy, searching for the gaze of Ama and Chehang. But, as it so often happened, the gods' eyes had landed elsewhere.

Several hours later, Sohmeng was woken abruptly by her own idiocy. She had never been a particularly sound sleeper, and had a tendency to flail around and hog every blanket that had the misfortune of brushing her side. This time, she had managed to roll onto her wrist, and all the splinting in the world couldn't protect her from the sharp zing of pain.

Gritting her teeth and grumbling curses, she sat up, cradling her arm. After the initial euphoria of surviving such an enormous fall wore off, she was left feeling annoyed by how easy it was to repeatedly re-injure herself. She sighed. No chance she was getting back to sleep any time soon.

All around her, the sãoni were out cold. Hei was nowhere to be seen—perhaps curled up with one of their reptilian siblings, or off doing whatever it was that Hei did. They hadn't exactly given Sohmeng an extensive list of their hobbies beyond screeching. She stretched, groaning softly as something popped into place in her back, and returned her gaze to the patches of sky above. If she leaned to the left, she could see Sodão Dangde clearly in the distance, the escarpment studded with soft luminescence. She hadn't been this close to it since before the Sky Bridge fell. It was surreal to see from this angle, a confirmation of how far she was from home.

How close she had been to being trapped up there now.

When the last batengmun had been selected, Sohmeng had been too young to join them by virtue of being born one day too late. At the time she had been furious, and nervous, too—she worried they might not be her friends by the time it was over. They would have a shared experience between them, she had thought, something private and powerful as the secrets of adulthood were unlocked. All the while, she would be in Fochão Dangde, staring forlornly at the Batengmun's Lantern glowing on the far side of Ateng. Missing out.

It had been a long time since anyone had seen that hopeful flame alight on Sodão Dangde. She certainly couldn't see it now. After the Sky Bridge fell, there was no way of retrieving the batengmun, no way of raising the Third Finger's portion of the Bridge to return them to the hmun. The children were left waiting, and party after party were sent to their deaths trying to rescue them.

No one was really surprised when the Lantern eventually went out.

Sohmeng stared hard at Sodão Dangde, searching for the version of herself that had completed her Tengmunji, that had been given the chance to learn the secrets of the mountains and come out whole. It was the same type of fantasy she had played through her mind since she was nine: she would emerge from her Tengmunji to find Grandmother Mi, who would pat her cheeks and sense the change that had come. In her heart, the first red sliver of Ama's eye would appear, lighting something that had not been there before. At last, time would begin to flow for her again. She would be kinder, and more patient, and less difficult. Easier to live with. Easier to love.

Of course, that wasn't to say she'd suddenly become meek or compliant—being a child of Par meant being impulsive, straightforward, contentious. By the hmun's own standards, if she wasn't causing a little grief, she wasn't doing her job. And honestly, Sohmeng *liked* Par. She liked the range she was given to argue, the roles she had access to as a woman. If she had been raised in Minhal...

Even on the floor of Eiji, it felt dangerous to consider. But it was hard not to wonder: what would her life be like if she had been allowed her Minhal birthright in Ateng? The hmun would probably gender her neutrally like the Chisong, Jāo, and Hiun phases, which would give her the freedom to move between men's and women's roles. But it would also come with the expectation of holding both masculine and feminine wisdom, which she definitely didn't have—godless night, her last good idea had nearly killed her.

So this is what it takes for me to reach you, she thought, smiling bitterly up at Sodāo Dangde. *A Tengmunji fit for a Minhal.*

The mountain stared down at her, unmoved. A dense void against the dazzling backdrop of the realm of gods.

But it wasn't fully void—there was that luminescence again, flickering brighter now. More than that, it was moving, blinking in inconsistent bursts.

Sohmeng rubbed her eyes with her good hand, clearing the sleep from them to get a better look; this time, when she saw the lights, she recognized colour in them. A purple pulse. Then a green. A purple. Two more greens. It reminded her of wovenstone gently illuminating the walls of a cavern, but it seemed to be shifting downward, moving closer to the base of the mountain with every passing moment.

She looked around for Hei, vague unease settling in the pit of her stomach. Maybe they could explain what it was?

"Hei?" she called, sitting up with a wince. "Hei the Elusive? Hei the Sleepy?" No response. The lights blinked brighter before disappearing into the thick of the rainforest below. "Hei of the Inconvenient Pee Break?"

Around her, the world was slow with sleep. The crickets sang and the thick vines above swayed in the wind. Sohmeng's heart throbbed in her chest. And across the grove, Green Bites rolled over in his sleep, exposing a throat pulsing and pulsing with a flickering emerald light that held all the warmth of the day, a warning of what precisely was coming to meet them at the foot of Sodão Dangde.

Nine

FOR A MOMENT, all Sohmeng could do was stare numbly into the darkness ahead. The enemy sãoni of Sodão Dangde were coming. She had seen them, she knew it, but when would they arrive? How long did she have? Fear hit her full in the chest; she stood as fast as she could, her body protesting every moment, to face the sãoni colony that had agreed *not* to eat her. A lot of good that truce would do if she got in the middle of a reptilian territory war. Where in two dark moons was Hei?

"H-hey!" she called, feeling immediately foolish. Naturally, none of sãoni moved, and her embarrassment yielded to anger at herself for holding back when this was actually life or death. She tried again. "WAKE UP!"

High above, a few night birds scattered, but the sãoni stayed huddled around each other, glowing throats to the ground, unmoving.

"No," Sohmeng muttered, reaching up and grabbing at her hair, "no, no, *no* I am not dying like this."

She stumbled over to Green Bites, giving him a hard thump on the side. She expected to be greeted with a faceful of cranky teeth, but he simply rolled over with a heavy huff, ignoring her. She ran to the next closest sãoni and was met with a similar reaction. Again and again she tried, until she made it to Mama. "Wake up, Mama!" she insisted, pulling on a head spine. "You have to wake up. Come ON, you stupid lizard!"

If Hei were here, what would they do? How would they wake the sãoni? Why did they have to disappear *now* of all times? Her throat itched with the urge to scream—

That was it.

Sohmeng paced back and forth, trying to remember the noise Hei had practiced with her, the alarm sound. With an apology to her vocal cords, she roared, releasing the ugliest noise she had ever made into the wild.

For the most part, the sãoni didn't move. A few stirred, but not enough to break them free of their cold-blooded snooze. That was the downfall of being an apex predator, Sohmeng realized—their biology never considered that something might dare to attack them. She screeched again and again, searching for the right tone, hoping that at least Hei might hear, wherever they were. Her next cry was so forceful, she nearly fell into the fire they had made for the jackfruit the night before.

And then she had a really, really bad idea.

Before she could think about it too hard, Sohmeng pulled a stick from the base of their shelter. She held it to the fire until it caught, and then lifted it to the tail of one of the vines above her head, thankful to be in a relatively dry season. Stumbling around the sãoni, she lit every vine she could reach—soon the canopy was garlanded in flame, releasing an urgent halo of heat and smoke. Her lungs scratched against it as the fire built upon itself, devouring every surface dry enough to catch. Knowing it was her last chance, Sohmeng inhaled deeply, and pulled from the back of her throat a bid for her life.

On the floor of the grove, a groggy green eye opened. Followed by another, and another. The sãoni stirred, looking around like so many sleepy toddlers as patches of burning vines fell upon them, small stings to amplify the growing warmth of the forest.

Sohmeng screamed again, in equal parts terror and triumph. Of course, the fire would lead Blacktooth's sãoni straight to them, but at least now they had a fighting chance.

Alerted at last to the trouble, Mama stumbled over to Sohmeng, nudging her with her face. All around, the other sãoni lifted their noses, shook out their glowing necks, and began echoing the alarm in one horrible chorus.

Sohmeng patted Mama's cheeks, speaking the only way she knew how. "They're coming, Mama. I saw them on the mountain, I—oh, godless night, you have no idea what I'm saying. You have no idea."

But this problem didn't last for long. The distant roar of sãoni was audible now. Mama growled, flattening herself to the earth, and turned to snarl sharply at the hatchlings on the ground. At once they swarmed up a tree, curling around each other like ink—and then Mama's nose jabbed into her side, prompting her to cry out and clutch it, grimacing. For a maternal creature, she certainly seemed to lack a sense of her own power. "I can't climb! My useless body already failed at being a bird, I'm not about to try my luck as a snake—"

The sounds of the enemy sãoni were louder now, the cracking of branches detectable alongside the terrible noises they made. They weren't even trying to hide their approach; it was an all-out war campaign. Sohmeng glared at the tree, trying to figure out how she was going to get out of this one.

From behind her, the alarm sound she had first initiated rang out, sharp and high and undoubtedly from a human throat. Sohmeng reeled around, facing Hei with murder in her eyes. "Where under the burning godseye have you been?"

"I was—" Hei stumbled to a stop, gawking at the forest. "Sohmeng Par, what did you *do*?"

"Wrong question," Sohmeng snapped, pushing back Mama's nose as the sãoni tried again to nudge her up the tree. "What you *should* be asking me is *What is that awful, nightmare-inducing noise in the distance?*" Right on cue, the bellow of a sãoni came rattling through the woods. Sohmeng didn't need to speak the creatures' language to know it was a battle cry.

"Blacktooth," Hei said, going pale beneath their makeup. Sohmeng could only nod, her heart beating so hard she thought it might burst inside her. Hei, normally so confident and unworried, was frozen in place; after a moment, they swallowed, pulling themself together and looking at her firmly. "Get on my back. I'll carry you up to the hatchlings."

With no small amount of difficulty, Sohmeng wrapped her arms around Hei's neck, grinding her teeth to keep from shouting. Hei made their way up the tree with their usual agility; it was only when they let out a few strained grunts that Sohmeng realized they were struggling.

"Are you okay?" she asked, suddenly concerned. She hadn't noticed any injuries when Hei came running back, but she'd been too distracted by the chaos to get a good look.

"Y-yeah," Hei wheezed, heaving the two of them up to a branch. "You're just . . . heavier than I thought."

Sohmeng snorted. Was this news? "You weren't complaining about me being fat when it was giving you something to snuggle on Mama—"

She was cut off by a particularly menacing roar out of the enemy sãoni. With one final push, Hei lifted Sohmeng onto an upper branch, where they stared anxiously down at the scene.

It was a sight to behold. Under the ominous crackle of the fire, Mama's colony of sãoni were clicking rapidly, a rolling, snapping noise like stepping on a thousand dried berries, their bodies pressed close to the ground as if building up the energy to launch themselves at the intruders.

And launch they did—as soon as Blacktooth's sãoni broke through, Mama's were upon them, snarling and snapping and shrieking as they tore into each other. Something heavy pressed on Sohmeng's leg; the hatchlings were climbing all over her, inviting her into their tangle. One reached a mid-leg to Hei as well, but they pushed it away, eyes locked on the fight.

All around them, the tatters of vines were burning up, changing the quality of the light faster than Sohmeng could focus her eyes. The trees were so bright they stung her retinas, and below, the world was a mass of tooth and claw and shadow and rage. For the first time since Hei had picked her up, Sohmeng was reminded of what the sãoni were: hunters, killers, an emblem of natural brutality.

Unfortunately for Sohmeng, two phases' time was not enough for her to distinguish sãoni the way she did people. She could recognize a few of Mama's colony from their distinct markings and personality traits, but from her current vantage point it was difficult to know which creature she should be sending her prayers to.

What she could see were the moons. The two wide eyes of Ama and Chehang were at full attention, boasting the divine wisdom of Chisong. Did the gods watch over sãoni?

Hei hissed loudly, lifting themself for a better view, body tensed as if they were ready to jump down into the action. Sohmeng reached for them, resting a hand on their shoulder. "What is it?" she asked. "What do you see?"

She followed Hei's attention to the source of their distress: a new sãoni had entered the fight, different from the rest. It moved slowly, slyly, skirting the edges as though it was searching for something. When it opened its mouth, Sohmeng could just barely glimpse in the fire-light the strangeness of its mouth—a corner of its teeth were blackened with rot.

Hei cupped their hands around their mouth, letting out three sounds, three cries of alarm spat out with the force of a curse: *Mama. Danger. Alpha.*

Being the alpha herself, Mama needed no warning, and wasted no time leaping in Blacktooth's direction, biting and snapping, swiping viciously with her claws at the other sãoni's eyes and sides. Above in the tree, the hatchlings squeaked and spat, writhing in Sohmeng's arms. Frantic at the sight of Mama in such close combat, she found herself yelling nonsense. "Get her, Mama! You can do it!"

With a kick of a strong back leg, Mama sent Black-tooth to her side and lunged to rip at her exposed belly. But Blacktooth turned, banging her own front claws into Mama's cheeks once, twice. She recoiled, trying to protect her eggs, and Blacktooth fell upon her, targeting her throat.

Hei let out a scream that had no trace of Sãonipa crackle. Distraught and furious, they yanked their hood up and leapt down the branches, plunging into the fray.

"Hei, NO!" Sohmeng cried, reaching for them instinct-ively. But Hei was already on the ground, yanking a sharpened stick from their shelter to serve as a weapon. All around, the warring sãoni were still entrenched in their own bloodshed. Hei was so small beside them, leaping and screaming and piercing any creature that dared separate them from their mother.

Another cry broke through the night, and Sohmeng watched in horror as one of Blacktooth's sãoni sunk its teeth into Green Bites' side. Hei was on them in an instant, shoving their stick into the creature's open mouth, straight through the back of its throat. It scrambled backward, gurgling horribly, and Hei ran to Green Bites, thumping his good side, their communication inaudible through the chaos around them.

Green Bites rose again, staggering on his feet and lowering his body to the ground for Hei. With another pat of encouragement, they jumped onto him, letting out a vicious cry and leading him toward Mama.

They darted in and out of the sãoni fights, dodging stray bites and claws and heavy tails. All the while, Mama squawked and writhed, using all her strength to beat Blacktooth back and protect her cheeks from the claws raining down on her. Hei guided Green Bites back to the shelter, grabbing two more pointed sticks as they passed, indicating direction with their voice and the lean of their body. When they finally came upon Blacktooth, the eldest children of their family's alpha, they came for blood.

Green Bites pitched into Blacktooth with a bellow, knocking her aside and digging his claws into the soft spot between her fore- and mid legs. Sohmeng held her breath as Hei vaulted off the sãoni, positioning themself in front of Mama with their pikes. And though they were small, they were fearsome to behold, the teeth of their hood glinting in the firelight, their body poised to kill. As Green Bites wrestled with Blacktooth, shredding her shoulder with his young, unrotted teeth, Hei kept off the rest of their assailants.

"Get up, Mama," Sohmeng said, pressing back against the tree trunk. "Get up!" Helpless though she felt high above the battle, Sohmeng had faith in Hei and Green Bites. The sãoni was vicious, relentless, and Hei—Hei's bravery in this battle appeared inhuman. She supposed that was the point.

With a ferocious roar, Green Bites sank his teeth into Blacktooth's neck and ripped, pulling out her throat in a spray of gleaming black. Seeing this, Hei released a series of cries, victorious and deadly, raising their blood-soaked arms to the sky. Around them, the fighting ceased for a moment, the sãoni echoing the snarls one by one.

It was interrupted only by the call of a large sãoni that had come in with Blacktooth's colony. In a flash, the others detached themselves from their opponents and hastily followed it into the forest, in the direction opposite to Sodão Dangde. Surprisingly, a few stayed, approaching Mama not with ill intent, but with caution.

Hei turned to Mama, nuzzling her face and stroking her head spines. Around Sohmeng, the hatchlings had climbed back down the tree, leaving her alone on the branch to watch the scene below unfold. She stared at Mama's torn, still form, praying up to her estranged gods that she would see the sãoni rise.

"Par," she whispered. "Par, Go, Hiwei, Fua, Tang, Sol, Jão, Pel, Dongi, Se, Won, Nor, Chisong—"

Tonight, it seemed, they were in a listening mood.

Mama lifted herself slowly, with a deep groan of pain, favouring her right side. Many soft clicks came all around the destroyed grove, and Sohmeng couldn't help but echo them in relief, in solidarity. With Hei on one side and Green Bites on the other, Mama approached Black-tooth's former sãoni who had not fled, and one by one they extended their necks, allowing a bite from her.

Just like that, the violence devolved into investigating, sniffing, rubbing cheeks. Sohmeng couldn't follow—had they really accepted their enemies into the family that easily? Was this the way forgiveness worked here? She couldn't say. She would have to ask Hei later.

Hei. A human who leapt willingly to their death without a second thought. Who stood beside Mama now, bloodied and exhausted, their face covered by a hood made from some other fallen enemy.

Sohmeng wanted to call for them, to ask for help down, but she could not bring herself to raise her voice. So she sat there, ruminating in her gratitude, smelling iron and woodsmoke and the flowers that ornamented the canopy.

Eventually, Hei came for her, carrying her back down with the kind of ease reserved for those who have not yet realized how closely they have brushed with death. Sohmeng was relieved to see none of the blood was theirs. Their black makeup had streaked down their face from sweat, or tears.

"We'll go to the river," they said. "See to our wounded. Sodão Dangde is our territory now, for as long as we choose to claim it."

Sohmeng thought this should be something to celebrate, and many of the sãoni were triumphant indeed, leaping and nuzzling where they could. Even Green Bites had a spring in his step, wounded as he was, and approached Hei multiple times to rub his face into their side. When he came to Sohmeng, she managed her fear of being up close with the gory face of a sãoni enough to stroke his head spines, earning a satisfied rumble.

Hei remained quiet, their eyes on either Mama or the ground as they approached the river. While the sãoni all rinsed off, splashing around and playing, Hei stayed on the banks with Mama, reaching into her cheeks and pulling out the eggs one by one, separating the broken from the whole. Mama watched them with her chin pressed to the silt, blinking slowly, resting her exhausted body. It seemed to Sohmeng that she wasn't terribly troubled by the loss.

But Hei was moved to weeping, their hands shaking as they put aside the cracked and shattered eggs. Soon they could bear no more, and simply sat beside Mama, sobbing into their knees, human all the way through.

TEN

THE SÃONI COLONY TOOK ITS TIME recovering at the base of Sodão Dangde, basking in the territory they had won from Blacktooth. Their victory did not take away from the breadth of their injuries; Mama spent much of her time resting in the mud by the river while Hei fussed and worried.

The battle had done a number on Hei; more than once, Sohmeng watched them get worked up as they attempted to care for the sãoni's wounds, pacing and squawking until tears came to their eyes. When this happened, Mama would take their arm in her mouth—more specifically, in the cheek pocket where she held her eggs. *You're my baby, too*, the gesture said.

In those first days, Sohmeng couldn't even imagine having the energy to worry. With her body in such rough condition from the fall, there wasn't much she could do other than sit and heal. The morning after the battle, Hei had approached her with a fistful of spiceroot, their eyes averted from her face as they explained that they had been searching for it when they heard her alarm cry.

"It brings down the, the *heat* in your wounds," Hei had said, wringing their hands. "Like when you're angry, and you feel hot in your face and your ears. The whole body reacts that way when you injure it. It gets angry."

Unsure of what to say, Sohmeng had pressed cheeks, quietly pleased to see the way Hei flushed in response.

Sohmeng's body, about as vindictive as the rest of her, was indeed holding something of a grudge. Even with the help of the spiceroot, it took ages for her to get a night of sleep uninterrupted by the stab in her ribs, or to pee without a throbbing deep in her bruised kidneys. Impatient as she was, she spent most of those waking hours just trying to stave off boredom without injuring herself any further.

"So are we just going to live here forever now?" she whined one afternoon after she had run out of rocks to throw. "I thought you said sãoni like to move around."

"They have a migration pattern, yes." Hei nodded, sharpening a stick for the new shelter they were building around Sohmeng. "But, like I also said, it's been interfered with. The colonies have been pushed further south—some of them are even starting to settle in one place. I imagine we'll do the same while Mama and the others recover." They paused, frowning. "It'll be rough on the local ecosystem. It always is when sãoni don't migrate."

"Why?"

Hei smiled self-consciously. "You've seen how they eat, Sohmeng Par."

"Okay," she said, poking at the shelter with her toe. "Then why bother settling at all? Why not just keep moving down the migratory breakfast line?"

"Would you walk your hmun into danger?" Hei shrugged, spearing the stick into the earth. The movement brought Sohmeng back to the evening of the battle, watching Hei ride Green Bites as they drove their makeshift pikes through the throats of enemy sāoni.

She swallowed. "I guess not. But ... I mean, they're sāoni. What could actually hurt them?"

"Humans."

Sohmeng snorted.

"I mean it," Hei said. "The humans of your hmun might not be strong enough to fight back the sāoni. But there are others who crossed the Great River, who came from outside the valley's network of hmun altogether." They spat disdainfully into the dirt. "They glimmer in the light. Poisonous as silvertongue."

Sohmeng was about to make fun of their complete melodrama when something caught her ear. "Wait, the Great River?" she said skeptically. "That's as far north as the hmun network goes. Do the sāoni seriously migrate all the way to the tip of the continent?"

Hei set down their work, brushing aside wood shavings to reveal the damp soil beneath. They dug their knife in, treating the earth as a canvas and scoring a rough map of the migration cycle. "It's a loop. Nearly all of the hmun fall along here, here ..." They tapped at points outside of the loop. "Safely outside the sāoni's range."

Sohmeng couldn't help but be impressed by the ingenuity of her ancestors—there was no way that the placement of all those hmun was a lucky accident. Long ago, when the ancient civilization of Polhmun Ão had collapsed, the surviving humans made the choice to split into separate settlements—small hmun which carried the legacy of the last great city the valley had known. It was thought to be safer, to have some distance from each other; if the resources were better distributed, they would not lose so many people should another great catastrophe arise.

Each hmun to itself, but all in harmony. When she was young, Damdão Kelho had told this story about a thousand times at the request of Viunwei, who listened with morbid fascination about the end of the world. It ached to think of it now.

Luckily, Hei interrupted her thoughts. "The sãoni aren't supposed to interfere with humans more than any other predator," they explained. "But when a great big hmun plants itself here—" They carved a deep mark at the tip of their map, then scribbled messy lines to signify the sãoni colonies scattering. "—it throws everything out of balance."

It was a difficult realization. No one had understood why the sãoni had rushed Fochão Dangde the day of the last crossing, or where the swarm had even come from. The traders were bewildered; the Grand Ones called it completely unprecedented. It had been easy for Sohmeng to create a story where they were nothing but monsters out for easy blood. Now, even with this revelation, her bias was hard to let go of.

It didn't really seem fair, when Hei's family were about as welcoming as sãoni could get. Sohmeng wasn't stalked so much as she was investigated, and Hei was entirely confident in both of their safety. Overcoming her prejudice came with a profound sense of dissonance.

"So if they got back on the migration route, everything would go back to normal?" she asked, brushing her knuckles over the top of the map.

"Time only moves in one direction, Sohmeng Par," Hei said with a queer, private smile. "But yes, it would help."

The longer Sohmeng spent in Eiji, the more her concept of 'normal' began to change. Her days played out beneath the misty shadow of Sodão Dangde, and as the phases passed overhead, the extraordinary nature of Eiji became ordinary. She spent less time gawking and more time appreciating. She watched magenta birds with great curved gullets swoop down the face of the mountain, seeking their prey. Much of nature, she came to learn, was an endless hunt, a tender dance with death. It took her less time than she would have guessed to adjust to it. Before long, the dying cries of the sãoni's meals had become ambient noise, blending with the other sounds of the jungle.

As her body repaired itself, it was easier to participate in her new life. In the mornings, she ate slices of bright pink guava alongside the birds' eggs Hei pilfered from nearby nests. When she was done, she'd spit the seeds to the expectant hatchlings, who made a game of gobbling them up. And while she couldn't help Hei with much of the physical labour needed to build their camp, she worked with whatever small tasks were given to her.

Between these tasks, she wholly dedicated herself to finding new and exciting ways to annoy some answers out of Hei.

"Okay," she tried one evening. "Important question: are we married?"

"Married?" Hei looked up from the sãoni skin vest they were sewing for Sohmeng.

"You said I was your mate. You know, when you bit me." She gave Hei a pointed look, but they didn't rise to the bait. Instead, they turned their attention pointedly back to their stitching. "Isn't that basically just marriage for reptiles?"

"It's not—I mean, not *exactly* ..." they stuttered, clicking uncomfortably. "For sãoni, it's mostly a matter of reproduction. Finding a mate who's going to produce healthy hatchlings, to strengthen the colony."

"Yeah, I'm still a few years out from thinking about kids." Sohmeng crossed her arms, leaning back against the tree and thoroughly enjoying the sight of Hei scrambling for an explanation. For someone who was so eager to rub their face all over hers, they sure were acting squeamish about this. "So where does that put me and you? Are we paired for life or what? Am I allowed to seek out other attractive, screaming lizard-people? Who's laying the eggs here?"

"I didn't—" They groaned loudly, rubbing their face. "I didn't want them to eat you, and I thought marking you as a mate would get you accepted into the colony! It was the only thing I could think of, and it worked, and—and it only needs to mean what we want it to mean. It doesn't have to mean *anything*, if that's what you'd prefer."

There was a jagged tension to the words, an agitated awkwardness. Sohmeng's initial instinct was to keep teasing, but she stopped herself, realizing that this might actually be important to them. If all the growling and biting was any indicator, Hei was truly invested in living as much of a sãoni life as possible, and marking a stranger as a mate might be bizarre for them on a level Sohmeng couldn't connect with.

Even in the hmun, she hadn't felt very comfortable with the bonds of romantic partnership. Sure, she experienced physical attraction to people, but the idea of meeting someone and just *feeling* some powerful unspoken connection sounded . . . a little ridiculous. In her mind, if she ever met someone who she actually wanted to spend her life with, it would be more of a pragmatic choice.

So she went the pragmatic route.

"Could it mean telling me how to gender you?" she asked. This sort of thing had never seemed like particularly personal information to Sohmeng—in the hmun, sharing pronouns was a given, and one's gender could be found based on their lunar name. But Hei remained tight-lipped as ever.

"Is there a reason it matters?" they asked with a sigh,

scratching at their mess of hair.

"Well, it helps me know how to talk about you."

"Ah, yes, to the wide variety of human beings you spend your days with," Hei bit back, rolling their eyes and tugging the sinew through the vest. Sohmeng couldn't help but laugh, pleased to see some progress in her mission to grow Hei a sense of humour.

"Okay," she nodded. "Fair. I guess it's more ... it helps me know how to think of you?"

"How to think of me," Hei repeated, leaning back against their tree and squinting at her doubtfully.

"Well, how someone's gendered can tell you a lot about who they are, what they do." Sohmeng shrugged. "I was raised in the feminine. Par, specifically—super feminine! I'm an arguer, direct. Even if my family didn't like it, they encouraged me to grow into it. So if you met me and I introduced myself as Sohmeng Par, you'd immediately know I'd be the first to disrupt a peaceful gathering if I had a problem. But if I didn't tell you, you might think I'm a jerk, or that it's personal."

Hei gave her a playful look then that implied they thought Sohmeng might just be a jerk regardless, and she was getting ready to swat them when they asked, "How do you think of me now?"

Sohmeng blinked, surprised by the question. She took a moment to consider what conclusions she'd come to about Hei, and gave her answer cautiously, not wanting to undo the success of actually getting them to open up. "I guess I gender you sort of neutrally. I'd use the 'they' pronoun."

"Why?" Hei asked, anxiety suddenly creasing their brow.

"Oh!" Sohmeng stumbled over her words, unsure what to make of the reaction. Was she wrong? Right? "It's not, I mean, I'm not assuming Chisong or Jão or Hiun or, or anything. It's just ... even if I don't know the temperament of the gods who watched your birth, you were born in a realm they both share? Like no matter what, both were somewhere in the sky, so honouring both of their influence with 'they' seems like a safe bet. Plus it's what the traders used to do when they didn't know so I thought maybe ..."

Hei had gone quiet as she spoke, their sewing forgotten in their lap. After a moment, they nodded slightly, looking to the sãoni seeking out fish in the river. A few of the hatchlings' throat stripes had developed in recent weeks, and they wore their emerging adolescence proudly, squawking up a storm as they splashed.

"Do you mind?" Sohmeng blurted. The reasoning behind assigning Hei the neutral pronoun in her head had seemed sound, but it worried her to think her good intentions might still have been hurtful. "Me thinking of you that way? Calling you 'they' with all those people I talk to?"

The corner of Hei's mouth flickered with a smile for a second, but they stayed silent, considering. At last, they looked to Sohmeng with an earnesty that made her heart squeeze. "I don't really think my gender is anything at all. But no," they said, nodding more firmly this time. "I don't mind being 'they'."

"You're more than just a pronoun to me, though!" She flushed the moment the words were out, realizing how intimate they sounded, particularly in the context of their discussion. Quickly, she followed it up with her closest approximation of Hei's sãoni name, hoping that would be enough of an explanation.

It was. The tentative smile on Hei's face broke into a grin, feral and playful, and they echoed the sound back. A chirp and three clicks, easy on their tongue.

Eleven

"OKAY BABIES," SOHMENG SAID, catching the moss-coloured egg she had tossed into the air. A dozen little eyes watched her hand, unblinking. "Let's see if any of you have learned a godless thing."

She steadied her feet, readied her arm, and pretended to throw her very best throw. The hatchlings went barrelling into the forest while Sohmeng cackled, shaking the egg still in her hand.

"Never gets old," she snickered to herself.

From behind her came a curious noise, and Sohmeng turned to see one last hatchling, smaller than the rest, without any throat stripes. The little sãoni looked from the egg to Sohmeng and back, tilting its head.

"Oh, you sneaky thing!" She crouched down, tutting in mock reproach. "Fine, it's yours. Size really isn't everything, huh? You just might be the smartest of the bunch."

The hatchling opened its mouth ridiculously wide for the egg, and Sohmeng laughed, stroking between the little nubs that would eventually become head spines. The hatchlings had provided her a source of entertainment during her long convalescence, and she'd grown fond of their antics. She chirped a friendly sound to the sãoni, who responded with a squeaky trill of its own.

"Sohmeng Par?"

Sohmeng looked up mid-chirp to see—

"Oh godless—"

—a hardly-clothed Hei returning from the Ãotul where they'd been bathing. She fixed her eyes determinedly on the hatchling, cheeks tingling. Hei was about as self-conscious as a toddler when it came to nudity, and brazen as Sohmeng was, she'd discovered that she had a certain weakness for well-toned weirdos.

"*Yes*, Hei the Stubbornly Nude?" she responded, patting the hatchling with newfound fervour.

"Have you seen my makeup?" They half-heartedly tugged on their sãoni skin top, leaning down to dig through the shelter the two of them had been sharing.

"You buried it under banana leaves so the babies wouldn't get into it." Not that it was helping. More often than not the hatchlings would stumble over, slick with charcoal and palmfruit oil, looking far too pleased with themselves. She reached back, pushing aside the leaves and handing the small bowl to Hei. "If you'd use some silvertongue, they'd leave it be."

"But if the smell stuck, they'd never go near me again." Hei clicked in gratitude nonetheless, and was just about to scoop up more of the concoction when Sohmeng swatted at their wrist.

"Wait, wait—you're seriously going to slap on more of that without cleaning off the old stuff first?" she asked, raising her eyebrows. Hei blinked, looking from the bowl to Sohmeng as though no one had ever mentioned to them that skin needed to breathe. For all Sohmeng knew, that might have been the case. "Feel your skin, you still have oil streaked all over! Weren't you *just* bathing?"

"I . . . rinsed it?" they replied, confusion wrinkling their brow. "But I didn't scrub it like the rest of me. I'm just going to be putting on more makeup anyway—" At Sohmeng's open disgust, their shoulders dropped in defeat. "Do I *have* to?"

"Do you want to keep squishing your face against mine?" Sohmeng asked matter-of-factly. Hei rubbed at their nose, which had very quickly gone pink, and nodded. "Then yes, absolutely, no question about it. Get up, we're going back to the river. Grab me a lime, too. Let's see what we can do about your hair."

"What's wrong with my hair?"

"Nothing's *wrong* with it, exactly," Sohmeng said, standing and tugging at Hei's wrist. "I just think you ought to get someone to cut it who isn't Green Bites."

"But Green Bites didn't—"

"Hei."

". . . Joking?"

"Joking."

They waded out to the large, flat rocks that broke up the river. It was one of Sohmeng's new favourite places;

the roar of rushing water all around muted the harsher sounds of the jungle, and at night she had a nearly open view of the stars that marbled the sky. Now she sat across from Hei, using a scrap of her old clothing from the hmun to scrub limewater and coconut shavings on their face. They scrunched their nose and spluttered, garbling out a series of unhappy growls.

"Oh come on," Sohmeng said, rubbing at their cheek. "You're acting like I'm killing you!"

"Washing's a lot different when—eghh!" They spat out a coconut shaving mournfully. "—when someone else is doing it!"

"Yes, yes, you're welcome for the help." Sohmeng inspected her work. Hei's eyes seemed to be permanently shadowed from the amount of charcoal they had smeared on over the years, but with the thickest of it gone, she could actually see how young they were. Nearly her age, perhaps a year or two older. How had she not realized this before? More importantly, how young had they been when they were exiled?

"I guess it does feel less sticky," Hei mumbled, touching their cheek suspiciously. As always, their eyes were striking, like the colour had been plucked from the jungle itself. But without the charcoal, they became softer. It was not a Hei Sohmeng was used to, and probably not a Hei that Hei themself was particularly comfortable with, but Sohmeng was grateful to be allowed a look, if only for a moment. They chirped, tilting their head at her, and she realized she was staring.

She cleared her throat, leaning back and looking at Hei with a critical expression. "So. The hair."

"It grows funny and then it sticks to the back of my neck when I sweat, so I just take a claw and—" They imitated hacking at it wildly from all directions. Which made a lot of sense, given what they were currently sporting. Sohmeng blew out a puff of air and fluffed her own recently-trimmed bangs.

"Alright, well. There has to be a better solution than that."

And so they found one. Sohmeng wasn't sure how long they spent there, laughing and shoving, dunking Hei's head to get out wash after wash of lime water. At one point, as she scratched at their scalp, she was pretty sure they were about to fall asleep in her lap. But in the end, with a lot of testing and the sharpest sãoni claw Hei had on hand, Sohmeng had shaved down the hair that troubled them, from midway down their ear to the base of their neck. She had done what she could to salvage the top, cutting it into something roughly consistent.

Hei rubbed at it, smiling nervously. "Last touch," Sohmeng said, leaning in to reapply the makeup on a much cleaner canvas. Hei's skin was soft, their breath warm against her palm as she smoothed the charcoal around their eyes. Their gaze was locked on her, vulnerable and dangerous in a way Sohmeng had come to know well. Regardless of the situation, Hei was an intense person, emotional and passionate and loud. Too big for a hmun. Familiar.

"Done," she said, more quietly than intended. Recovering herself, she pushed her face back into a smile. "Now *that's* what I want my mate to look like."

Hei flushed at that, seemingly unsure of whether they wanted to puff out their chest or dive headfirst into the river. Sohmeng smirked, pressing cheeks with a face that was no longer covered in grime, and found that Hei returned the press with unexpected force, leaning to meet her. They pulled back just far enough to break the skin contact, just close enough for both of their noses to touch. Sohmeng swore she could hear Hei's heartbeat thrumming in the air.

"Sohmeng Par," they said, breathless, and it sounded almost like a question.

"Just—Sohmeng." For once, she didn't have it in her to lie. "Call me Sohmeng."

The kiss was clumsy at first for its eagerness, at once sweet and feral, like biting into ripe fruit, or splashing through the river, or laughing herself breathless. Hei leaned her back against the stone, their solid weight a delightful pressure against the flesh of her belly—she grasped at their back, felt their muscles gone taut with want, a charming contrast to her own boneless glee. When Hei at last broke the kiss, startled and a bit delirious, their hair was back to looking like so much bewildered fern.

Sohmeng covered her mouth, laughing out loud at the sight of them. It was a nervous sound, mostly, but a good one too. She could feel where her own face was smeared with charcoal and oil, but she found she didn't mind.

After a moment, Hei laughed too, looking at Sohmeng as though there were a treasure map hidden somewhere on her face.

Their brow suddenly creased with concern. "Was that—was that alright? Is that, are you, is—"

"Hei, would you do me a favour and take a good look at my face before you fully commit yourself to panicking?" Sohmeng said, stretching out underneath them with a happy hum. "How do I look right now?"

"Beautiful."

Good of them to notice. "Firstly, it should be a crime to be that sweet. Secondly, you're full of it, I'm totally covered in your face-gunk." She gave them a little pat on the cheek, wiggling out from under them.

"Do you mind?" they asked shyly.

"Being covered in your stupid face-gunk?" She pursed her lips, pretending to consider. "I mean, I guess it's worth it if I get to be close to your stupid face." She grinned at them, and they returned the look, toothy and unselfconscious. It really was a stupid face, wasn't it? Stupidly attractive. "Come on, we should head back. I'm hungry and I don't want to end up eating you by accident."

"I'll get some trout from downriver!" Hei said, leaping up eagerly. "We can glaze them with the orange-flower nectar I've been saving! Go start a fire, I promise I won't be too long. I want to, for you, I want—" They gave up on Hmunpa, letting a happy trill say everything for them, and went hopping along the boulders down the river.

Sohmeng watched them go, wondering how she could possibly hold so much fondness for one person. And though she knew the fire should be made sooner rather than later, she took a moment to lie on the boulder and feel the warmth of the sun sigh down through the leaves and sink into her skin.

So that's what kissing feels like, she thought. *Not bad at all.*

Up in the hmun, initiating that kind of physical intimacy was strictly the privilege of adults. While Sohmeng had harboured plenty of interest, it had been infuriatingly forbidden to her. Technically, since she had never completed her Tengmunji, she still had no business doing it now.

But did Ateng's rules apply to someone who was flourishing in Eiji? Who had begun to build a life there?

Because it had to be said: in recent weeks, Sohmeng had begun to think of the colony of sãoni as a hmun. As *her* hmun. When she watched Green Bites try to impress a violet-throated sãoni by dragging a shouting Hei around by their leg, she responded with laughter instead of fear; when the hatchlings swarmed her for playtime, she often found herself carrying them around. She had even taken to napping with Mama. The mind-boggling concept of life below the mountain had transformed into something pleasantly mundane.

Then there was Hei. Getting to know them hadn't been easy. They clearly wanted to connect with her, but they shied away from behaviours they deemed overly-human. On top of that, their moods could make them downright recalcitrant when rubbed the wrong way, and Sohmeng wasn't exactly the pinnacle of tact. Setting each other off had been a regular, predictable affair early on.

But things had changed. For all the two of them could butt heads, they each made an effort to listen to the other, to try better next time.

Now, as far as mates went, Hei was nothing to shake a yellowbill at. They did what they could to provide Sohmeng with good meals, and tolerated the faces she would pull when trying something new. The first time Sohmeng got hit with her period, Hei wasted no time seeking out a fluffy, absorbent plant for her to wrap in fabric. And though they'd complain when Sohmeng squirmed around in her sleep, nearly knocking them into the fire pit on multiple occasions, they never left her alone for bed. When Green Bites got too energetic about teasing her, Hei would wave him away, snarling a boundary on her behalf. They cared for her, and were patient with her, and did what they could to compromise when challenges arose.

Maybe Sohmeng hadn't entered the realm of adulthood, but she felt pretty confident that the two of them had earned the right to kiss. And even if the hmun disagreed, she really wanted to try again anyway.

The heat of the sun-warmed stone tingled in her hands, Chehangma's divine light sinking into her. Was it praise or rebuke? She had always had trouble discerning the two. She sighed loudly, sitting up and stretching. A walk would help clear her head. Leaving behind the river, she pushed her way into the jungle, mindful to steer clear of treacherous tree roots and dangerous, thickly-scented flowers.

It wouldn't be difficult, Sohmeng thought, *to stay with the colony.* It would take no effort to give up returning to the hmun, to let her family move on with the assumption that she was lost. But things were complicated by the fact that her camp was currently parked quite literally in the shadow of Sodão Dangde. It loomed over her, a heavy reminder of what she would be turning her back on. And now that she was almost done healing, she was running out of excuses to avoid thinking through her options.

Before the Sky Bridge fell, Sohmeng had spent just under half of her life in Sodão Dangde. She remembered the darker, woodsier smell of the moss, the unmistakable whistle of the wind tunnel in the sunrise side. It held the house her father had preferred, without the slanted roof of the Fochão Dangde house that he constantly whacked his head into. It was the mountain she had been born in. And it was likely full of the corpses of children she had grown up with.

Or maybe it wasn't.

Every attempt to send members of the hmun to the First Finger to repair the Sky Bridge had ended with their being devoured, unable to retrieve the batengmun left alone long past their Tengmunji's end. It was unsettling to consider for too long. Jinho's cousin had been among the batengmun, a promising girl of the Mi phase. Sohmeng remembered overhearing a conversation between him and Viunwei one night, Jinho's soft voice breaking as he spoke: "Well, if they aren't dead, we can certainly say the batengmun reached adulthood tenfold, can't we?"

The only hint that they might have perished was the darkened Lantern. While the superstitious hmun might have read the worst in that sign, Sohmeng wasn't ready to take it as definitive proof. And here she was, the first from Ateng to walk Eiji since the fall of the Bridge, as good as family to the sãoni that could get her up there.

What would happen if she discovered the fate of the batengmun once and for all? If she returned from death to help the hmun raise the Sky Bridge? If anything would be enough to change the hmun's perception of her, that would certainly be it. And while she wanted to say she no longer cared what the hmun had to say about her, while she wanted to free herself of the need to find her place in a social structure that didn't want her, it wasn't that easy.

She rubbed at her face. There really was no such thing as a fresh start, was there?

Life in the world below was good. She was happy, and cared for. But before she bound herself fully to Eiji, she had to resolve what loomed in Ateng.

When she shared her thoughts with Hei that evening, they didn't exactly share the sentiment.

"Absolutely not," they snapped, storming around the grove with Sohmeng following behind.

"Hei, listen, I know you don't like talking about the hmun—" She was cut off by a vicious snarl from Hei, who tossed aside the soapstone they had been carving when she first presented her idea. It thunked off a nearby tree, sending the monkeys in the middling branches scurrying and attracting the attention of the sãoni. Hei didn't notice, busy as they were pacing and being difficult. "I understand this is a lot to ask, but—"

"Aren't you happy here?" they blurted, turning to face her with hurt in their eyes.

"What?" Sohmeng frowned. "Hei, of course I'm happy! I make it pretty clear when I'm miserable."

"Then why do you want this?" Hei gestured to Sodão Dangde in one sharp, angry motion. Sohmeng rubbed her face, trying to grasp what 'this' actually meant to Hei. The hmun? The answers? Humanity? She hadn't expected them to react warmly to a proposal to climb the mountain, but neither had she anticipated the extent of their distress. It had been a while since they had fallen apart this way. "Why do you need this if you're happy here?"

"I'm greedy, I guess?" Sohmeng cringed. Not a great time to be funny.

"I'm your *mate*," Hei said, their face twisted in pain. "We—I thought we were . . . I mean, this morning—I know I, I'm not very . . ." They struggled with their words, their tension building until they shouted with frustration. Mama perked up her head from across the grove, growling at Sohmeng, who responded with a few appeasing clicks. This got Hei's attention, and they softened slightly, hopefully, before they dropped their gaze. "We're supposed to stand by each other."

"That's not the same as forcing each other into situations we don't like," Sohmeng insisted, waving Hei's words away before they could argue. "No, please listen to me—I'm not saying you have to rejoin the hmun, or even go into the caves at all. I'd like you to come with, obviously, but I wouldn't demand it of you, because I'm not actually that unreasonable! But I—I *do* need your help getting up to the entrance. I can't do that alone." She swallowed, gritting her teeth through the vulnerability that rose from within her. "This is really important to me, Hei. And if you won't go with me, I'll—I'll just have to figure something out. Find a way to get better at climbing so I don't fall off a second mountain."

"Don't make jokes about that," Hei mumbled, wiping their eyes. Their hands trembled, but their voice was calmer.

"I'll joke as much as I please," Sohmeng teased, gently taking their shoulders in her hands. "You're my mate, right? This is how you stand by me. Help me out. I'm not—I'm not going to run away from you. I'm not just looking for an excuse to leave."

For a moment, Hei only stood there, still as one of the trees. They glanced up once, with a face like they had a whole world caught under their tongue, a story they needed out before it poisoned them. And then it was swallowed down, put in the place where they held all of the other things they didn't know how to say to her.

"We climb the mountain," they murmured at last, not quite meeting her eye. "But only once you've healed completely. I'll show you what you want to see, but I'm not breaking my back dragging you up to it."

Sohmeng's heart nearly stopped right there. She let out a laugh that caught on itself, reaching forward. "Hei, thank you—"

"Don't—" Their voice was sharp again, but their eyes were as gentle as she had ever seen them. "Please don't thank me for this."

Unsure what to say to that, Sohmeng switched to their preferred language: a pressing of cheeks, a bumping of noses. Hei softened, releasing few soft clicks like the skipping of stones, but Sohmeng couldn't have said what they meant in Hmunpa. She wasn't sure that they were hers to understand.

Part Three:
Sodão Dangde

Twelve

DRENCHED IN THE PLUM AND tangerine light of late afternoon, the valley really did look like the domain of the gods. Eiji was its own creature, wild and tangled with snarling, sprawling life, but nothing was quite like the view up in Ateng. Now that she wasn't plummeting to her death, Sohmeng found it a lot easier to appreciate.

However, that was challenged by the fact that she was currently attached to a lizard who was scaling the cliffside as if gravity was more a suggestion than a rule. She clung to the sãoni she called Singing Violet with a white-knuckled grip, teeth chattering with the effort of staying conscious through her terror. Hei had used their replenished supply of sãoni skin to fashion something akin to a saddle with steadying leg straps; theoretically, she was safe. Remembering Jinho's assurances about the safety of egg collecting, Sohmeng held on a little tighter.

When Hei had talked about using the sãoni to get up Sodão Dangde, Sohmeng had, like an idiot, assumed it would be at a more leisurely pace, perhaps around the significantly more forgiving sunrise side. Green Bites screeched in delight, outright vaulting to another part of the cliff despite the very small and human Hei holding onto his back. For all that Hei could try to guide the sãoni, they weren't the alpha; it was incredibly lucky that Green Bites and Singing Violet were following Hei's direction at all.

Chunks of the cliff gave way to Singing Violet's scrabbling claws. *Luck,* Sohmeng thought as she ducked, *is a pretty relative term.*

To her left, the Third Finger was visible in the near distance. She couldn't tell if it felt auspicious or ominous to peer so closely at the lifeline to Sodão Dangde. Eventually, as they rose, she would be able to see the Finger's portion of the Sky Bridge, left curled and untended after all this time. How many nights had the batengmun spent at the mouth of the cave, staring at the Lantern that burned on Fochão Dangde, waiting for their half of the Bridge to rise? At least as many as Sohmeng had spent simmering in her cot, wishing she had been there by their side.

A loud whistle pulled Sohmeng from her thoughts; Hei had released one hand from Green Bites, pointing at a massive column of mist. Sohmeng sucked in a breath between her teeth—watching Hei fall to their death would be a poor start to their adventure.

"What is that?" she yelled to them, leaning back as far as she dared to get a better look. Thankfully, the two sãoni found their way to a narrow ledge; it was refreshing to be horizontal again.

"Waterfall!" Hei called back, the adventurous look in their eye a welcome break from the unhappy, skittering glances of the past week. "I'll bring you!"

Her parents had told her about waterfalls before. Other ground-dwelling hmun lived around them, villages who traded the rich fruit of Eiji for the ever-glowing wovenstone of Ateng. It never failed to amaze her, just how much was contained in the rolling hills of Eiji, separated like sacred strata: the clear sharp blue of sky, the milky mists, the verdant canopy, the shout of upper life, the murmur of lower, the sweet dark smell of the soil. All of this without even considering the influence of the spirit-building moons, the life-giving sun.

She stared down at the waterfall, imagining it pouring from the mouth of some great, ancient god. Another layer to unpack. Another world to discover.

Eventually they reached the midpoint of Sodão Dangde, a deep cave pockmarked in the sunset side. As the sun slipped below the horizon, the sãoni began to lose their heat, and Hei didn't want to risk them going sluggish when the cliffside cooled down. This wouldn't have been an issue if they'd left in the morning like Sohmeng suggested, but Hei had been reluctant to leave Mama, who remained in Eiji with the rest of the colony, and Sohmeng hadn't had the heart to hurry them along.

Far back in the cave, Green Bites and Singing Violet curled around each other. Sohmeng glanced at Hei, who was rolling their shoulders as they took up their own spot near the entrance; feeling her gaze, they looked over their shoulder at her and tentatively patted the ground beside them.

"Missed me?" she teased.

"Yes," they answered, contemplating the valley before them. Their forehead was creased with gentle, worried lines.

Sohmeng waited a moment, wondering if they were going to say something more. The two of them had already hashed out their conflict as much as possible; they had come to their agreement. It seemed all that was left was to sit in the discomfort of it.

"Things are probably going to keep feeling a little weird until this is done," she said as she joined them. It felt good to admit this out loud, to stop pretending like things were fine.

"I—" Hei hesitated, then nodded. "Probably."

"You want to . . . talk about it?" Hei scrunched their nose, and Sohmeng couldn't help but laugh in relief. Some things were still the same. "You want to kiss some more?"

Hei paused, considering, and then nodded once more with a tender, affirmative click.

Later that night, they lay snuggled together at the mouth of the cave, stargazing. The lunar phase had just shifted into Tang, with Chehang at its brightest while Ama journeyed to darkness. It was different seeing the moons like this, with the whole world open, as opposed to constrained within the sacred skylight above Chehangma's Gate.

She shifted closer to Hei, her fingers hard at work untangling their hair, nails lightly scratching at the base of their scalp. They sighed against her, chirping into the soft fold in her neck, undoubtedly smearing even more charcoal all over her. She didn't mind.

"You know," she said, watching the moons, "this is actually a pretty auspicious phase for what's going on. Chehang is really, well, open I guess. Open to change. And Ama is learning to give up some of her control." She readjusted her head on the pillow of her arm. "It's why Tangs can be difficult—they're super compassionate, but they're really reluctant to change anything that disturbs their worldview. And they can get so passive aggressive."

Beside her, the muscles in Hei's neck had stiffened slightly, their body tensing against some invisible force. It struck Sohmeng that they might be a Tang, and she backpedaled quickly, not wanting to spoil their evening.

"I mean, I like them though!" she continued quickly. "My brother, Viunwei, his boyfriend is a Tang." She tried to stop herself from babbling, but her mouth had different ideas. "At least, I hope they're still together. It was weird before I left, they had a lot to work out, but maybe me falling off a cliff was good for them? Viunwei is a Soon so he responds to everything so dramatically, and Jinho Tang would definitely want to be there for him even though he was being a huge jerk before—"

"You know a lot about this," Hei said suddenly.

She stopped her detangling. "I mean, yeah? It's important."

"Important." There was something biting about their tone, a dismissiveness that set Sohmeng on edge.

"It helps me understand my place in the world," she said, trying not to sound too defensive. "It helps the whole hmun. I mean, that's why we all study phasal influence, isn't it? The phases lay out our roles, they bring ... social clarity, I guess. You know, when the gods' will is interpreted fairly."

A beat of silence passed between them. The sky suddenly seemed cramped to Sohmeng, the moons bright with judgement. She bit the inside of her cheek, frowning at them. She probably didn't have much right to follow the phases as closely as she did, given what she was, but studying them felt like a good way to make up for it.

"Who determines what's fair?" Hei asked, propping themself up.

"What?"

"Who chooses? Who makes these rules?"

"I mean, Ama and Chehang—"

"No," they interrupted, shaking their head. "No, the gods have their moods, but the ... the people determine how others should be treated. How they should act. Have you ever considered that people might behave certain ways because they're trained to from birth? You're a Par, so you're going to argue. Your brother's a Soon, so he's going to be a leader. Would either of you be that way if you hadn't been told so your whole life?"

"What are you getting at?" Sohmeng could sense her body gearing up for a fight. Pounding heart, heat in her hands—it was bizarre, how similar it felt to what she experienced when she kissed Hei. She crossed her arms, closing herself off as the old familiar curtain of dismissal shut on her.

"Maybe it doesn't matter." They shrugged, not meeting her eye. "Maybe the phases don't have to mean anything."

So many times, the hmun had rejected Sohmeng for not being mindful enough of the gods' will; now here she was, being pushed aside for considering them *too much*. The dissonance made her uncomfortable, as though she was suddenly some sort of advocate for the traditions of the hmun that had rejected her. And yet she found herself defending them, anger winning out to reason.

"They mean something to me," she said tersely.

"Does it help you, though? Does being called Par really make you feel like you belong?" This wasn't something she wanted to answer. It wasn't something she had an answer for. It was too much, to have her confidence be tested, to be seen so thoroughly by someone who wasn't even trying. "Is there really so much harm in questioning—"

"Not all of us are rushing to abandon our hmun, Hei!" she snapped, and instantly regretted the words.

Hei's eyes widened a fraction; their chest crunched inward as though she'd driven her closed fist into it. For all they made a show of not caring about the hmun, of treating it with disinterest or disdain, Sohmeng had experienced that reaction enough times herself to know it stemmed from hurt. Rejection. She felt stupid a dozen times over—Hei was an exile, and here she was, throwing it back in their face. A lot of good that auspicious Tang phase was doing her now.

"Hei, I'm sorry," she said, rubbing her arm, trying to wipe away the harm she'd caused. "That—that wasn't fair."

Hei said nothing, tucking their knees to their chest like a child bearing the same old scolding. The light of the moons stopped just in front of them, never quite touching.

"Really," she tried again, "I was—I was out of line." A memory arose: a roomful of heavy sighing, the disappointment on her brother's face— "Completely out of line."

"But it's okay, right?" Their words were sharp with sarcasm, harsh with hurt. "It's expected, because you're Par. It's just in your *special nature*, and I should let it go because the gods say so."

Sohmeng clenched her fists, stung. She deserved that. "No. I'm telling you I was unfair, and I'm apologizing—"

"You know what?" Hei stood, their jaw clenched, assuming that intimidating predator's stance they wore when they were on the verge of tears. "I'm glad that I'm hãokar. I'm glad they don't want me. I don't want them either. And I don't want apologies from someone who's never understood what it's like to be outcast in her *life*."

Sohmeng wanted to be the bigger person, to take their righteous anger with humility and show the balance that existed within the Par phase she was meant to claim—but she couldn't. She couldn't be something her brother was proud of. She couldn't honour her parents. She couldn't be initiated. She couldn't be enough.

And suddenly she was done pretending she ever stood a chance against herself.

"*Minhal!*" she shouted, the word echoing through the caves, bouncing off the sleeping sãoni. Hei froze where they stood, stunned, and Sohmeng felt nearly sick with hurt at the horror on their face. They didn't care about the phases, apparently didn't even believe in the will of the gods, and yet they were still afraid of her. But as always, she couldn't let it go. "Sohmeng Minhal. That was—that was my name for the first hour of my life. I was an accident, come early, determined to, determined to be *trouble* from the start. My grandmother lied for my parents, called me an early Par, and the village was so busy getting ready to cross to Fochão Dangde that they just accepted it. They let it go, and I lived, and I was raised in Par."

She stepped back to the edge of the cave, allowing the light of her estranged gods to fall upon her. She should have been afraid, should have cowered in the dark, and yet she was only emboldened by her admission. *Try me,* she thought furiously. *Push me from the mountain a second time. Prove your disdain, show me how terrible I really am.*

"I didn't even know it until I was eight, when I started studying the phases. I asked so many questions, and my father was acting so strangely and my mother was so frustrated with him and then she—she just told me. She told me, because she thought I had a right to the truth. Like a real Par would do." She laughed, feeling the tension like a knife in her throat. Hei watched from the shadows, silent. "My Grandmother Mi was on her side. She said that it would be in the hmun's best interest to let the tradition of exiling go, but that they weren't *ready* yet. So I lied. And my parents died. And the Sky Bridge fell. And I couldn't be initiated. And when I tried to prove I belonged, I was, I was *thrown from the mountain.* So don't tell me that I've never been an exile!"

She wasn't sure when she had started crying. It had never been her preferred method of releasing pain—most of the time, she just shouted until she felt better. But here she was, breathless and weeping and staring Hei down like it was the last day of her life. In a way, it was.

It terrified her to admit this. It felt so good that she didn't know what to do with herself. These feelings warred within her, moons at odds despite all their phasal promises. Chest heaving, she stared at Hei, searching for a response. For disgust, or compassion, or validation. But as always, they were an enigma to her, their eyes averted like a shamed warrior, one arm wrapped around themself. She clenched her fists, burning. Wanting.

When Hei finally spoke, they didn't have much to offer. "I'm sorry for what I said, too." It came out muted, anticlimactic. Deeply unsatisfying. Apparently even the hãokar couldn't escape the influence of Ateng, couldn't release the caution and tradition they had been raised in. Her heart hardened around itself as she wiped her eyes, searching for barriers to build.

That's it? she wanted to ask.

"It's fine," she said.

More silence. Hei seemed at a loss for words. It made Sohmeng feel very, very tired. "Let's just go to bed, alright?"

Her voice was soft, not easily recognizable as her own. She shifted back into the cave, nodding Hei over, wanting to warm herself where her skin had suddenly cooled like sãoni at dusk. They approached her carefully, fidgeting, and lay down beside her. For once in her life, Sohmeng didn't have it in her to argue.

It's not what a Par child would have done. It's not even what she would have done that morning. But Sohmeng Minhal had always wanted to please the gods that had forgotten her, so she closed her eyes and settled close to Hei, heavy with her own quiet exile.

Thirteen

SOHMENG AWOKE THINKING she was still in Fochão Dangde. It must have been the air, blanketed in cool damp, untouched by the sunlight spilling into Eiji. As her ears caught the soft, rhythmic drip of water from somewhere in the cave, she half-expected to hear the murmurs of the hmun preparing for the day's activities along with it, to see Viunwei fussing over his reflection in a vanity bowl. Instead, what she saw were the sãoni, throats still glowing as they stretched their necks toward the sunnier parts of the cave. She sat up blearily, orienting herself as she kneaded at her sore neck.

Hei had already risen and was sitting against the pair of sãoni, stroking their flat noses. For all they had been angry last night, spitting out their hurt like rotten fruit, they appeared to have simmered down overnight. Their fingers traced around Singing Violet's eyes in a rhythm that seemed to soothe the great creature as much as Hei themself.

Her stomach flipped; that's right, the sãoni were staying here. They would be hiking the rest of the way on foot. She wasn't exactly eager to get back on Singing Violet, but neither was she looking forward to being alone with Hei. They might have slept off their upset, but Sohmeng didn't feel much better upon waking, and the idea of making such an intimate journey together felt nearly intrusive. Not that she ever had a shot of navigating the mountain alone.

She tugged at her bangs in frustration—when had she become such a coward? She had never been one to avoid confrontation in the past, even if it was bound to result in ugliness. So what was her problem?

She recalled a conversation from many phases ago: *I was raised in the feminine. Par, specifically—super feminine! I'm an arguer, direct.*

Reality weighed heavy in her stomach. She wasn't able to claim that sort of truth anymore. Perhaps it hadn't ever been hers to begin with, but last night she had finally admitted it to herself and another, in full view of the gods.

She had no place in Par.

Having spoken it aloud, she felt suddenly torn from a part of her identity, without any way of understanding what truths of her remained. While she had to admit there was something freeing about Hei's idea that the laws of the phases were arbitrary, giving it too much power made her feel tremendously off-balance. All she had ever known were the divine mathematics of Ama and Chehang; if the numbers were meaningless, what was left? Without that structure, how could she know who she was, where she belonged?

She straightened her shoulders. She supposed she just had to decide for herself what kind of person she was going to be today.

"Hey," she called, snatching onto the first instinct that whirred by her. "What's for breakfast?" At least for now, the truth remained that she was still obnoxious.

Hei kept stroking the slumbering sãoni. "I thought we might forage as we walk. Fiddleheads grow well in the high mists. If we're lucky, we can bring some back down by the end of this."

"Or share them with the batengmun," Sohmeng said, standing and rolling her neck, "if they're not dead."

Hei rested their hands in their lap, not offering a verbal response. Sohmeng had gotten familiar enough with their silences to know that this was a reaction to something external rather than something from within. Were they judging her as callous? Because, well, she was. But they had never seemed to mind it much before. She tugged her bangs again, irritated by her overthinking. Godless night, she was acting like Viunwei.

"Come on," she said, nodding Hei over. "Before Green Bites wakes up and bullies you into a belly rub."

Making the climb was no easy task. Sodão Dangde's terrain was unpredictable, full of loose schist and sudden drops. On top of that, the yellowbills continued to take their territory very seriously. But when Sohmeng actually glimpsed the number of nests tucked into the cracks in

Sodão Dangde's cliffside, she was dumbfounded. Without the hmun to farm the mountain, the ecosystem had been allowed to flourish. Logically, she knew that was the primary reason for the hmun's cyclical pilgrimage anyway. But seeing it up close was a reminder of how many resources humans required to survive, and of how effortlessly the rest of nature got on with itself regardless of disruption.

A broken rope, and the hmun faced extinction. An infestation of humans, and the birds just flew elsewhere. How dangerous it was to depend on the goodwill of the world around them, to put their lives into the hands of such precarious structure.

It made her wonder what value the structures had in the first place, if it was so easy to knock the feet from underneath them. Maybe it was a matter of keeping faith in an illusion, seeking comfort in perceived safety. After all, when the Sky Bridge fell, there was honour placed upon explorers and shame upon the hãokar, despite the fact that they were being sent to their deaths either way.

She ran her fingers along a rope of sturdy, flowering vines, giving them a light tug. They were springy, with a waxy texture to them that she could easily envision dried into fibrous strands for ropemaking. Her ring glinted in the light, a wink of silver against dark slate and petals the colour of sunrise.

When she had fallen, it felt deserved. Unfair, but earned. Losing her hmun was frightening and destabilizing, but there was a sense of expectation there. When you swing carelessly from a rope, it is likely to snap. When you push the laws of the hmun by advancing before your time, the laws will push back. When you spend sixteen years lying, the consequences are bound to be catastrophic when you're discovered. Maybe she didn't like what had happened to her, but there was a sense of logic to it that helped her survive it.

Ahead, Hei was combing through a massive fluffy fern for any hidden fiddleheads; Sohmeng squatted beside them, assisting in their search, still considering. It hurt more to lose something you had chosen rather than something that was imposed. It was easier to fail at someone else's game than to mess up one of your own making. Perhaps that was the value of the hmun's rigidity—with rules to follow and consequences to expect, even pain was predictable. Now, as she walked with Hei from a place with no law but the food chain, it became clear that loss meant something very different when you lived a life of your own design.

Did Hei feel like they had lost something last night when they learned Sohmeng was Minhal? They had been nervous all day, restless in response to Sohmeng's relative calm. It was an odd role-reversal. As they continued their ascent, Hei only got more anxious, emitting aggravated grunts and missing what was right in front of them. Sohmeng had never been the better forager of the two, but here she was, the travel bag around her thigh stuffed full of food while Hei had hardly found a thing.

Suddenly, Hei stopped in their tracks. They turned in place, chewing their lip. "What is it?" Sohmeng asked, peering around them. She couldn't see why they were hesitating; the path continued just fine. A relief, after several harrowing boosts over head-high boulders.

"This isn't—" They pushed around the foliage that hung against the wall of the mountain. "There's a, a thing. I can't find it."

"What kind of thing?"

"It's a, a slot, sort of. It's not—I thought it was here." They crouched down, digging through the bushes with distracted hands.

"A slot, sort of," Sohmeng repeated, crossing her arms. Hei's descriptive language left a lot to be desired. "Can you give me anything else? Maybe I can help you—"

The short laugh that came out of them was uncharacteristically bitter. "I don't know how you could possibly help me with this." It would have been insulting, if some instinct in Sohmeng hadn't alerted her to the fact that it wasn't personal. All day, there had been a wildness in their eyes, the cautious and bedraggled look of an animal at the end of a hunt. At first, Sohmeng guessed that they were still raw from last night's fight. But now, when the time had come to stop moving and all of Hei's nervous energy was forced to stillness, it was clear that something greater was rattling them.

"Hei," she said, crouching beside them, but they recoiled from her as if she had stung them. "What's going on? You've been acting funny all day. I know last night was hard and . . . and I'm sure I haven't exactly been the best company today—" They were shaking their head, giving Sohmeng that look they got when they choked on their language. She took their arms gently. "No, stop it, I don't want to argue about whether or not I'm difficult to be around. I don't care how much you like me, you don't get to lie and say I'm pleasant." She smirked at Hei's exasperated huff, their bewildered hiccup of a laugh. It was a good sign, if she could still make them laugh. She squeezed their forearms, encouraging them to pay attention. "So, just—talk to me? As best you can? Maybe sit down while you do it so you don't flail yourself off the mountain? That's sort of my signature move, and I'm going to get really annoyed if you take it from me."

"Plenty of creatures fall off the mountains," they said shakily, sitting down beside her and leaning against the wall they had been scratching at. "Careless baby lemurs, for example—"

"You know, when I said talk to me, I wasn't asking for the world's saddest story," Sohmeng said, resting her head on their shoulder.

"It's not sad, it's just nature."

"Well, it seems to me that nature can be pretty sad sometimes."

Hei trilled softly at that, running their fingers along a sāoni claw sewn into their sleeve. The claws were pretty intimidating when Hei was running at someone, Sohmeng mused. But sitting here like this, all they did was emphasize how small their hands were in comparison. Sohmeng wondered what sãoni the claws had been cut from, how many tries it had taken Hei to get their needle through.

"There is ..." Hei began, tilting their head back, eyes straight up the side of Sodão Dangde. Sohmeng reached to touch the claw they were fidgeting with, waiting. "There are many things I want to say to you. That I have wanted to say to you for a long time. And last night, I—" Their eyes flashed with pain. "I should have. I didn't. I was scared, and I hurt you, and I'm sorry." That was when Sohmeng realized there had been a grave misunderstanding between them.

"Were you scared of me ...?" she asked, working around the words with embarrassing caution.

"No," they insisted, gripping her hand in theirs. "Never. Well, maybe sometimes when you first wake up." Sohmeng laughed, and Hei's eyes wrinkled at the corners. Their hand was tense in hers as they strained against the effort of speaking. "Last night, I was only scared of myself. And what you might think of me, for what I am."

"What, a sãoni?" Sohmeng shrugged. "I've gotten used to that. I like it about you."

"I—" Hei paused, stunned into silence, and Sohmeng realized they'd probably never heard those words before. After all, human company wasn't easy to come by in exile. She shrugged again, nuzzling them gently. In typical Hei fashion, they chirped softly. And though it was in no human language, Sohmeng understood. Eventually, they found their words again. "When I first found you, I thought I would get you in one piece, bring you to a nearby hmun in the network, drop you off, and return to my life with my family. But I . . . I marked you, and I got to know you, and I didn't want to take that back. And then it felt like you had marked me, too. And like you didn't want to take it back, either."

"I don't," Sohmeng said, her heart squeezing as she admitted it. She still wasn't so sure what love actually meant—sãoni matehood was a mystery to her, but honestly, so were the complex rituals of Ateng courtship. Neither of them fit her experience exactly; divinely-approved promises of everlasting devotion sounded about as unreasonable to her as biting someone to save their life.

Sharing these feelings didn't have to change their relationship. It was enough to know they wanted to be near each other, and respect each other, and see each other like they had not been seen before. They could work out the nuance as they went.

Hei let go of a breath they must have been holding for a very long time, nodding and allowing their back to uncurve itself. When they spoke, they sounded more confident than Sohmeng had ever heard them. "You showed me yourself last night. And I want to show you me, too. I want to be brave. And I want you to stay with me, and be my mate, and talk to me while I'm busy doing other things, and nearly set me on fire in my sleep. I want to kiss you, and press my face into yours. I want to walk all of Eiji with you, the whole migration route, and bring you to waterfalls. I want to find a single fruit that you'll eat without making faces at me first, and then I want to bring it to you every day, and see that you're happy. I want to be something that makes you happy." They stared off the side of the mountain as though they were building this future before their eyes, laying the foundations of their new reality. "And I . . . I can't do that without being honest. It wouldn't be right."

"Then be honest," Sohmeng said, as gently as she could muster.

"I'm so afraid." The words came out barely a whisper, the skin beneath the scales. Sohmeng had no comfort for that, no reassurance. Speaking hard truths aloud was painful; their fear was perfectly reasonable. They sighed, running their hand through their hair with a scowl. "And I can't find the, the *entrance*. It's been so long since I was up here, and I'm scared I don't remember anymore."

"The entrance?" Sohmeng tilted her head up. "I thought it was higher than this."

"No, not that one. There's, there's another. A different way in."

"Okay, so how do we find it? I take it there's not a great big sign on the front door?"

"It's hidden," said Hei, resting their chin on their knees. "It's through a slot in the rock face behind a cluster of vines, these flowering vines. I used to shred them to make thread, they're the strongest thing I have besides sinew. I think they were used for building the Sky Bridge."

"Wait." Sohmeng perked up. "What colour were the flowers? Sort of orange-ish? Pink tipped? Look either like a snack or an easy way to die mid-squat?"

"Yes! That—first, no, they aren't edible—but that sounds like them. When did you see them?"

"A while back. You had your whole head stuffed in a fern."

"Really?" Hei stood up, brushing off their legs and looking back the way they had come with an expression that would have been wistful if it weren't for the anxiety drawn up in it. "I thought it was so much further up."

Time moved slowly as they went back down the mountain. The urgency in the air gave way to something smaller, nearly shy. When they reached the vines, Hei let out a tender hum, and Sohmeng knew it was the right place. They exhaled, nodding to themself, and pushed back the thick curtain of greenery to reveal a thin slot in the sandstone, just as they had said.

"This way," they murmured, and though Sohmeng could see the way their body was tense with fear, the way their face was drawn with resignation, she could also see the determination in their eyes. They stepped through the slot, and she followed.

As the two of them shuffled sideways through the entrance, Sohmeng found herself in greater darkness than she had seen in a while. The feeling was at once serene and claustrophobic, and she was about to ask Hei if they should have brought fire when the walkway widened, and the gentle glow of wovenstone fell upon them. Sohmeng blinked rapidly, trying to adjust her eyes to the change in light. Familiar, but distant now. It was hard to believe that it hadn't even been a full cycle since she'd begun her life below.

"This was one of the exits for the traders," Hei said, gesturing toward a set of stairs carved into the mountain. Sohmeng felt a pang of strange nostalgia. Her parents probably walked those stairs a dozen times in their life. "It was the lowest point to the ground they could get before climbing the outer mountain."

Sohmeng was about to approach the stairs when she noticed Hei turn, following a thick vein of wovenstone with their fingers. She had assumed they would appear out of place inside Sodão Dangde, given they were so at home in the jungle, but she saw now that it was quite the opposite. When they turned to face her, her breath caught. Their eyes were as much the colour of the canopy as they were the deepest slices of wovenstone. For a moment, it was like seeing Sodão Dangde itself, meeting its solemn, holy gaze.

"This cavern connects to many cave systems. Some of them were used by the hmun, but many were deemed too narrow, too unstable. Easy to get lost in." They stepped around a great slab of stone, peering into some darkness beyond. "It's where I grew up, after she hid me away."

Sohmeng went cold.

"What?"

"My grandmother," Hei said, their voice impossibly tender. They were unwavering as they turned to Sohmeng, as though their doubt had sensed the judgement of the mountain and found itself undeserving. All that remained was Hei, open and honest and afraid, brave only by choice.

"Heipua Minhal. It was the name the Grand Ones spoke upon my exile. It was the name she called to me in the dark."

Not even the wind dared to brush past the vines and disturb the truth that Hei had spoken. They offered a hand to Sohmeng, who could think of nothing to do but take it. Together, they crossed over the threshold: two dark moons, liberated from the gaze of all uncompromising gods.

Fourteen

"**EIGHTEEN YEARS AGO,** I was born at the height of First Minhal. '*Under stars many as my wrinkles and night moonless as my left pupil.*' My grandmother's words." Hei ran their fingers along the veins of wovenstone, following their intricate patterns by touch alone. It was an act of familiarity, of homecoming. Just watching it made Sohmeng feel like she was imposing, and yet she did not avert her gaze. "I was a loud crier. Still am. My parents never could have hidden me until Par. They weren't traders like yours, they had never been to Eiji. They had no chance of surviving their exile, and they knew it. So when the day came for them to walk from the hmun with me in their arms, they carried a blanket full of fruit and called it Heipua Minhal. My grandmother said they were very graceful."

Nausea prickled Sohmeng's chest. She remembered the stories her own grandmother had told about the last Minhal child Ateng had seen, stories told to scare her into following her role as Sohmeng Par—it was Hei.

It had always been Hei. How long their lives had been intertwined.

"How...how did you survive?" she asked, her voice barely a whisper.

"Grandmother harvested mushrooms all her life, deep in the caves. People were used to her absence. And after her family was exiled, no one asked questions when she wandered, or disappeared for some time. No one suggested she sleep alone in her house, and her singing didn't bother anyone when it was low in the ground. They were patient, assuming she had lost something of herself." Hei peered around a corner, half a smile flickering on their face. "But they were wrong. She had found me." They tilted their head as though they were listening for something, and then slipped into the dark, their little finger hooked around Sohmeng's. "Do you know her? Esteona Nor."

Of course she did. Esteona Nor had been a sad and strange fixture in the hmun for years. Kind but confused, prone to misidentifying every brown-eyed, female-shaped person as her daughter, patting their bellies and making people avert their eyes in discomfort. Dead for five years, now. Numbly, Sohmeng nodded.

"She raised me in the parts of the mountains most were too afraid to walk. And even then, she encouraged me to go further, to make a home for myself in Fochão and Sodão both. I would bring her the biggest mushrooms I could find, and she would imitate how the villagers reacted when she brought them to the communal meals.

It made me proud, to know I had been helpful." They ducked around a block in their path, then slipped down a narrow passage, navigating confidently even when they passed through a part of the cavern with no wovenstone for light. "Maybe you ate one of my mushrooms." Their voice rose hopefully at the thought, and for the first time, Sohmeng recognized that very specific lilt as a longing for approval, all-pervasive and thick with a need to survive.

"Maybe I did," she said.

"There is so much food in the caves, you know. If you're small enough to crawl, and you know where to look. I would catch armour bugs the size of my fist." Hei sensed Sohmeng's reluctance as they entered another patch of darkness, and gave her pinky a little tug, bringing her closer. The walls had become tight around them, suited for a child's slight frame. Sohmeng had to walk sideways, and even then it was a tight squeeze. "I couldn't under-stand why the hmun had to cross mountains when there was so much bounty in each one. Grandmother Nor said there were just too many people, but it made no sense to me. I had never seen them, not everyone. A couple times I got close to the main hall, but I always had to find somewhere dark and quiet to go after, just to get all of the noise they made out of my head. I don't know how they all bore it every day."

"I won't lie, it gets grating," Sohmeng said, and then immediately winced at her petty complaint. But Hei only smiled, squeezing her hand again with a hum. "Were you ... were you ever lonely?"

"Yes. Sometimes I missed my grandmother. Or I would hear a conversation between two harvesters, and wish I could join. Or even just listen, maybe while one of them patted my arm." They chewed their lip as they slowly let out an admission: "I snuck in close to watch the people sometimes. No one was looking for me, so it was easy to blend in, and I was good at hiding. But seeing everyone together made me feel lonelier than being alone did. Is that strange?"

"I don't think so," Sohmeng said, considering her own experiences of feeling outcast. It was not the isolation that hurt as much as the knowledge that others were allowed to be together. "It's harder to enjoy yourself when you know you're missing something, I guess."

The passage broadened then, allowing the two of them to walk single file. Sohmeng kept close behind Hei, who led her to a stack of boulders that could have been described as stairs. They pressed at the stones cautiously with their foot, seeking the safest path possible for Sohmeng to follow.

"When I asked my grandmother why I couldn't join the rest of the hmun, she told me the truth. She warned me that they would throw me out like they had my parents, and then I would never see her or the mountain again. I would be hãokar. And I loved the mountain, and I loved her, so I stayed in the caves, and I loved them too. The only time I left them was for the crossings."

"Wait, you made the *crossing*?"

"My grandmother and I did it together. I climbed into the bag on her back and made my body very small, and she carried me across the Bridge. She moved slowly, but everyone assumed it was because she was frail. She wasn't. She was never frail." Their voice positively trembled with pride, and Sohmeng felt, perhaps for the first time, the depths of their inherited strength.

"Crossing the Bridge was terrifying, and wonderful. I would peer through the seams in the fabric and see colours so bright it hurt my eyes. Even through her bag I could, I could feel the sun. But I never got the full view the rest of the hmun did. Not until I found the exits." Hei glanced over their shoulder at Sohmeng, and the cloud of some old worry cleared from their face, yielding to their own brightness. Their speech picked up like the feet of a child, nearly stumbling with eagerness. "Fochão and Sodão Dangde both have them, you know. Not just the mouths of the trade routes, but small pockets at the end of some of the cave systems. The mountain goes porous in places, and you can sit at the edge and reach your hand into the whole world."

Hei's fingers flexed in Sohmeng's hand. She thought of the view from the cliffside, the way her teeth had chattered so hard with involuntary laughter that she'd barely heard Jinho speak. It was strange, how easy it was to imagine Hei facing that view with fearless serenity.

"Sometimes I sat there for hours. I would miss meetings with my grandmother, and she would worry, and I felt bad. But when I was up there, I saw—I saw *everything*." Their voice was breathless, their footsteps echoing through the elevated halls of the cave. Sohmeng could hear a roost of bats chittering with annoyance from above, but Hei paid it no mind. "Grandmother said the mountain range was the hand of a very old god. And I don't know if that's true, but if it is, then Eiji is its body, all connected in a perfect system. Life touching life touching life. And death, too. All of it, all together, perfect." They turned with sudden speed, so close to Sohmeng that she nearly jumped back. Their eyes searched hers, darting back and forth, full of the same sort of hunger she saw when they kissed. "Do you see it? The system?"

"I . . ." Sohmeng struggled to respond, wanting to give them what they needed, unsure if she could do it honestly. "I don't know, Hei."

"It's alright," they said insistently, taking both her hands in theirs, "if you don't see. The hmun's systems would be clearer to you, they're all you're raised to understand. But when you walk away from the, the *structure* and the lunar law—when you see the moons without the eyes, the phases without the superstition, when you look at the crossing and stop thinking about the entry into Par long enough to notice all that has grown in your absence—"

Sohmeng thought of the eggs, nearly overflowing from the nests on Sodão Dangde. She inhaled the soft, sweet decay of the mushrooms that had grown all throughout the caves. Slowly, she nodded. "The perfect system."

Hei's face broke into a smile, nearly silly in its wideness, its wildness. "The perfect system," they repeated. With a last squeeze of her hands, they turned to resume their climb up a particularly steep ledge. "Humans have their place in it, of course. We're animals, we belong. But no human-powered system can ever overrule the one we were born into. That's where we make mistakes. It's where we cause harm to everything around us, force things out of balance so the system has to fight back. And then we bemoan its brutality. It isn't right."

The hushed intensity of Hei's voice pierced into Sohmeng, opened her to a new image of the two of them: the exiled, the outcast, the too-much children. Cut out like cancers from the hmun, and yet still alive and thriving. If they could flourish under a godless sky, who was to say they were inauspicious?

It seemed to her that strength was a hallmark of Minhal, its survivors made sturdy from necessary ingenuity, made caring by a careless community. She reached for a hand-hold to pull herself up the side of the cave, feeling only the faintest ache in her healed wrist. Fractured, but not broken.

At the top, Hei reached to pull Sohmeng up. Thankfully, the cavern had opened back up into a space where they could move comfortably rather than duck and crawl and pray they wouldn't get trapped. For a while, they walked in silence.

"Things changed when—" Hei hesitated. "When my grandmother died."

"I'm sorry," Sohmeng said softly.

Hei let out a few stiff clicks, wordless; Sãonipa had always been the language in which they were most themself. It surprised Sohmeng, how relieving it was to hear the sounds return to their tongue. That was the Hei she knew.

"I waited for her in the caves, in the same alcove I always did. But one day . . . she didn't come. I was twelve." Sohmeng remembered that day. Esteona Nor had been found slumped in front of her dinner bowl, peaceful and still. The other Nors prepared her body and carried it to the opening of Sodão Dangde to be laid before the gods. They sang her favourite songs at dinner, playing surrogate family to the one Esteona had lost. The animals took care of the rest, freeing the soul from its weary shell.

"I think maybe she knew it was coming," Hei said. "She had been behaving strangely in the weeks before. She moved slowly, and stumbled on her words. She said things that scared me: I was getting too big to carry across the Bridge, the caves would not be so kind to me in adulthood, I needed to have my Tengmunji. I needed to become part of the community. She was contradicting every warning she'd ever given me—I didn't know what to make of it. And then she was gone, and there was no one else to ask." Hei reached out to touch the wovenstone, an old anchor. "Death is part of the design. I know that now, and I do my best to honour it. But it was difficult, back then.

"I thought I knew what it meant to be alone, back when Grandmother Nor was alive. But I was wrong. As long as there is one single being who loves you, whose life is entwined with your own, there is purpose. But without it, everything is—hollow." Their voice caved in around the word, mournful and ragged. Sohmeng took their hand, saying nothing. "I do not know how long I was alone for, after that. But one day, I noticed that things were quieter than usual. First Par had come, and the hmun had crossed to Fochão Dangde. All that was left were the batengmun."

"And you," Sohmeng said, pained. She remembered the morning of that terrible birthday, the way she had sulked as she held her father's hand, scowling and kicking pebbles. While she was moping that Viunwei would be her only playmate, Hei was hiding in the caves. Another Minhal, trapped.

"And me." They nodded, some old ghost of determination flashing in their eyes. "And I thought, I was the right age, wasn't I? My grandmother had said I couldn't stay there forever. And I thought I could—I could watch them, gauge their personalities, see who I might want to be friends with. And maybe, if I could be brave, I'd go introduce myself. They were young. Perhaps they would be more flexible than the Grand Ones my grandmother had warned me about. If I just made myself useful and showed I was no danger, they would accept another hand to help them. When our Tengmunji was complete, maybe they would appeal to the Grand Ones to welcome me, argue the virtues of having a Minhal child present." They shook their head, their voice dropping. "Of course, it took nearly two whole cycles before I came out of the caves, and when the batengmun saw me, I almost ran right back the way I came."

"They must have thought you were..." Sohmeng trailed off, unable to imagine the scene. A group of children huddled around a fire, trying to coordinate their social roles for the next two years, interrupted by a face in the dark. She was amazed that the more tenacious of the batengmun hadn't tried to kill Hei on the spot. "I don't even know."

"Mm." They looked at her, eyes still shining, eerie against the black of the caves, the black of the charcoal they wore that made them so animal. So invisible. "When they moved past their panic and I found my voice again, I explained my circumstances. Some were sympathetic, others wary. A few were downright hostile—Tansen Se suggested that they throw me from the mountain, and it was probably what rescued me. He had always been so quick to judge, to lash out. No one wanted to side with that and look irresponsible. Maio Chisong and Dimanhli Ker were the ones who made the argument for me to stay, and Maio's word had weight. Two bright moons to compliment two dark. They thought it could be auspicious. As for Dimanhli...well, I think she just felt bad for me. She was the one who held my hands when I started crying."

How strange it was, for Sohmeng to hear her childhood playmates named aloud. The hmun didn't speak of them much during their Tengmunji—it was custom to allow them to reside on the opposite mountain without physical or spiritual interruption—and after the Bridge fell, and the Lantern went out, they were referred to as one great entity, the lost batengmun. Going name by name was too intimate, too painful. And yet Hei spoke of them with familiarity, bringing back every memory Sohmeng thought she had forgotten.

"That sounds like Dimanhli," she said, thinking of the girl who invited everyone into her games, who refused to eat armour bugs because she thought they were cute. Her throat felt tight, and though she wanted to say more, she couldn't. She took a shaking breath, reminding herself that there was a chance they were still alive. What would she say if they were? She, who had stayed back in the hmun while they were trapped in isolation?

"It took time, but when the vote came, it was in my favour. So I stayed. I made friends, my first friends, and I lived with them for six more cycles, following the practices Maio Chisong suggested. They were a leader, through and through. Noble. When Tansen Se called me unlucky, they would scold him and tell stories about magic shadows. That's what I was to them, I think. A shadow behind their double light." There was not a touch of bitterness in their voice. If anything, they sounded tender. "It was easy, being a shadow. I got bolder. I showed my hmun where the best foraging was, and where the spring water sprouted from wells in the mountain. And they taught me their songs, and speculated about who I would be allowed to marry when the hmun took me in. Dimanhli Ker said I'd be the first Minhal Grand One that Ateng had ever known, even though I would only be fourteen." Sohmeng heard their voice waver. She blinked quickly, clearing her eyes, holding their hand as they walked, straight-backed, through the passageway. "For six cycles, I belonged."

"And then?"

"You tell me, Sohmeng Minhal." They stopped at another steep climb, turning to face Sohmeng under the light of the wovenstone. Now, she could see the hurt in their eyes, the confusion. Not directed at her, but at a time long past, and everything that had followed as a result. "The first day of Par came upon us, and no one arrived. Then the next, and the next. Then Par was complete, and entered into Go. And Go into Hiwei. Hiwei into Fua. Fua into Tang. At first we figured there had been an accident. Then, we considered that it could be a test. Come First Won, we started thinking it was a punishment."

"A punishment?" Sohmeng asked, bewildered. "But Hei, no, it was the Sky Bridge, the link to the First Finger—"

"How were we supposed to see that?" Hei retorted. "With a line of mountains in front of us? With no word from the hmun? We knew nothing of the Sky Bridge except for the fact that on our end, it was still rolled up in full view. No one came for us. And that had never happened before." They turned back to the wall, searching for a way to climb. "Just as a Minhal had never been initiated."

Sohmeng grabbed their arm, turning them around, refusing to let them bear this story alone as they had borne everything else over the years. She didn't care if it gave them the distance they needed, if it helped to mask their shame. She was selfish, and she could not handle the idea of a child spending one more night alone in these caves. "That wasn't what happened."

"I know," Hei said, their voice gone hoarse. "But we didn't know then. All they could do was search for what was different, and I—there I was. But again, Maio argued for their shadow. They said I was as much a part of the hmun as anyone else. And I was useful—no one knew more about the mountain than me. So again, they cast a vote. I was even allowed to participate this time. Despite Tansen's venom, which some of the others had begun to share, the majority decided for a second time that I would stay. A second act of generosity for the year and a half we had spent together." They made a sound that was more a sob than a laugh. "It protected me for a cycle more before a fight broke out. A bad one. Maio Chisong was cut down where they stood with a hunting knife, in the middle of a shouting match with a group of the others. Tansen started it, but I don't know who it was that took out the blade. And Dimanhli just screamed and screamed, she said Maio's death had doomed them all, they'd held all the wisdom of the moons and now—"

Their voice broke in full, words dissolving into tears and heaving breaths. The noise echoed throughout the caves, ricocheting off every surface until the world positively rattled with the sound of their despair. Sohmeng took Hei's arms, trying to steady them as they sank to the floor, trying to swallow her own horror at the thought of the children she had grown up with turning into the greatest tragedies of Tengmunji. It was no use. She thought of Dimanhli Ker's sensitivity, Tansen Se's loud jokes over dinner, the charm in Maio Chisong's haught-iness, Edmer Heng's hair that curled only on one side, Foão Mi's skill with her dice. Thirteen batengmun left behind that crossing, left to their possible deaths. At the very least, to the death of their best selves.

She remembered Viunwei's hard eyes when he returned from his own Tengmunji, his insistence that she would only understand when she, too, became an adult. She thought the ritual was meant to grow people stronger, to help them understand what they could offer to the community. She had never considered what it would do to those who, when left alone to look at themselves, found that they hated what they saw. How fortunate she was, that her own isolation had only galvanized her will to live. She held Hei close, chirping into their hair, until they were soothed enough to speak.

"They did not vote again, after that," they said, breaking the silence with great pain. "I was sent down the trade route we entered from, out onto the side of Sodão Dangde. I didn't dare return to the caves. I had already showed them my best hiding spots, and I was so afraid to be found. I had watched the way Maio crumpled, the way the blood pulsed from them, and I . . . I could not shadow them into death. I didn't want to shadow anyone, anymore. I didn't want to know anyone ever again." They closed their eyes, resting their head against Sohmeng's, holding her hands like Sohmeng had gripped the ropes on Fochão Dangde. A lifeline. "I walked down and down and down, and I was scared. I had made excursions outside before, but I had never tried to live there. I didn't understand what food was safe, and the sun was so bright, and the rain—the first time it rained, all I could do was wail at the feeling all over my skin. I thought it would never stop, that I would melt away into nothing. The sãoni must have heard me crying. Or smelled me. I still don't know."

Sohmeng's heart squeezed in vicarious terror. She had gotten so used to the idea of Hei as a part of the sãoni that she had never stopped to imagine what it must have been like to be found as a child. The closest thing she could imagine was her own experience: all those teeth, the unsettling clicking, the certainty of death.

"Mama came then. Blacktooth, too. Back when they were still in the same colony. They cornered me in a cave to eat me, and I knew I was going to die and I just—screamed." Hei smiled at the word, laughing with a strange and powerful pride. "I screamed, as loud as I could. Not in terror, but in—in *anger*. And then Mama screamed back. And I screamed again. Back and forth until I spat pink. And then she came over to me, and I readied myself to die and—her cheek, she pressed her cheek against my belly. Her face on mine, nearly knocking me over. She, she *chose* me, Sohmeng." The tears returned to their eyes, but they were still smiling. They ran their thumb over a sãoni claw, a comforting motion, and made the noise that Sohmeng had come to know as their name. *Hatchling Food. Baby Dinner. Heipua Minhal. Strange Human. My Child.* "When Blacktooth moved on me, Mama fought. She scooped me into her cheek, and I yelled and cried until I realized she wasn't eating me. And then I was at the bottom of the mountain, slimy and bruised and surrounded by sãoni that answered to Mama, now."

Quietly, Sohmeng called their name in Sãonipa. She was no Mama, but Hei pressed their cheek to hers just the same.

"They raised me," Hei said softly. "And soon, it wasn't so hard to be out of the mountains. How could it be, when I had the entirety of Eiji? There are other mountains, and waterfalls, and rivers, and trees so thick you could live inside, if you spent a life hollowing them out. I missed Grandmother Nor, but I had an entire family, and all of the beauty in the world, and there was no name to hurt me with, no rules to kill me but the laws of nature. And I could abide dying by those. One day, I will."

Sohmeng hooked a finger around their claw. "The perfect system."

"The perfect system."

Sohmeng wasn't sure how long it was that they sat on the floor of the cavern together. At first the silence was daunting after the overwhelming power of Hei's story. Then, it was soothing. And then, Sohmeng realized that it wasn't silence at all. Far away, she could hear water running, and the rustling of bat wings, and the skittering legs of some crawling creature, and the last breath of the wind reaching and reaching into the lungs of the mountain. Life was everywhere. And death, too. Though she could not put a word to it, Sohmeng had become aware of something greater than herself, but that also was herself. Her and Hei and the entire world.

For once, Hei spoke first. "Once we climb this wall,"

they said, "we'll have only one short passage before we enter the main cavern. If any of the batengmun still live, they'll be inside."

"We don't have to go," Sohmeng said.

Hei frowned, clearly confused. "But—"

"We don't," she repeated. "Not if you don't want to."

"We've come all this way," Hei began, straightening up, but Sohmeng shook her head, feeling the same passion building in her chest that had gotten her scolded so many times back on Fochão Dangde. Too bold, too arrogant, too willing to cause disturbance for the sake of addressing unchecked needs. "If we turned back now, you wouldn't know—"

"I don't care," she said. "I don't care, Hei."

"The, the Sky Bridge. You wanted to see if—"

"Later," Sohmeng insisted. "Or I'll find another way. I'm smart."

"But you said you're my mate and—"

"That means neither of us gets to force each other into situations they don't like."

Hei stared at Sohmeng, scanning her face as they tried to compose their thoughts. Sohmeng met those eyes head-on, gathering herself to do what she did best: say what she meant, no matter what. "It doesn't matter how far we've travelled, or what the plan was, or how badly I thought I wanted this. What the batengmun did to you was wrong. And you know, I don't care that they were scared, I don't care that it was a difficult situation, I don't care that they were my friends. All of that can come later. Right now, I care about how *you* feel, because no one else seems to have ever taken that into consideration." She turned to Hei, cradling their jaw in her hands. "If you don't want to do this, we can turn back right now, and I won't be angry. I won't even be annoyed. Okay?"

As always, Hei did not respond immediately. It usually bothered Sohmeng, how long it took to get a reply out of them. But she was thankful to know they were not rushing thoughtlessly into this decision. They tapped their sãoni claws, clicking nervously, their racing thoughts apparent on their face, until at last they found their answer:

"I want to go," they said slowly.

"Yeah?"

"I want to go," they repeated, more certainly this time. "I don't know why, maybe I shouldn't, but I—I want to. Is that bad?"

Sohmeng let out a long sigh, leaning her forehead against Hei's. For a moment, she just rolled it back and forth, grateful for the soothing pressure as she pondered their question. It didn't take long, and when she spoke, the words came without shame or guilt or uncertainty. A victory for any being, human or not.

"Honestly?" she began with a laugh, "call me selfish, but I've always thought that *wanting to* is the only actual good reason to do anything."

"You're selfish," said Hei, a smile on their face.

"You too." Sohmeng bonked their foreheads together, running a hand through Hei's hair in one last gentle gesture. "Let's do this."

Fifteen

ALL WAS STILL in the main hall of Sodão Dangde. The
fires were long dead, and cobwebs were draped like lace-
work between the small stone homes. No sounds played
against the cavern walls; no smells of supper cooking
permeated the air. It was dreamlike, uncanny.

From the moment she entered the cavern, Sohmeng
knew that nothing had been alive in there for a very long
time. In some ways, it was a relief to finally release any
hope that still lingered. It didn't make it any easier when
they found the bodies.

Four of them, curled atop thick dark stains, reduced to
heaps of tattered skin gone slack over bone. Their hearth
was ash and their dinner bowls were unwashed. Sohmeng
was able to look at them for about a minute before she
turned and was sick on the ground, her own insides rattling
in response to having seen what they look like on another
person. Hei crouched beside her, holding back the hair that
had come loose from her bun, rubbing her back.

179

"G-godless night," she cursed, closing her eyes against the image of what—*who*—lay behind her. "They're—I mean, I knew they were, but . . . you can't even tell who they *are*."

Hei looked over their shoulder at the bodies. "Dimanhli's here," they said after a pause, strange pity underlying their sorrow. "Furthest left. That's her bracelet. Her older sister gave it to her for her Tengmunji, she wouldn't have lent it to anyone."

Sohmeng's stomach lurched again, her throat raw from the acid. She had known death before—it was part of life in the hmun. She had even participated in the sky burials of other Pars, a thing she felt conflicted over to this day. But she had never confronted bodies this way, especially not the bodies of people she had known growing up. She took Hei's hand, grateful for the grace with which they were responding. Eiji was full of death and everyday violence, a constant string of casualties in the endless fight for survival, the food chain in perpetual motion. She supposed the hmun wasn't so different, with their stolen eggs and roasted armour bugs and wovenstone hacked from the walls. The cruelty was a part of life, deemed acceptable for the new life it fostered. The thought didn't do much to ease the pounding behind her eyes.

"That could be Sohtei Won. Or Pikong Ãofe?" Hei said quietly. "I'd have to get closer to be sure."

"In, in a minute, I just—" Sohmeng cut herself off, clutching at Hei's shirt. She blew out a slow breath, thinking of Jinho Tang, tearful at the thought of his cousin. "Is Foão Mi there? Can you, is she ..."

Hei said nothing, taking their time observing as best they could from where Sohmeng was keeping them both. "Second to the right," they said with gentle certainty. "The small one. That's Foão."

The closure felt hollow. Shouldn't it have been a good thing, to have this answer at last? "She's my, my brother's, his boyfriend's—" Sohmeng stopped, attempting to pull herself together.

Par, Go, Hiwei, Fua, Tang, Sol, Jão, Pel, Dongi, Se, Won, Nor, Chisong, Heng, Li, Ginhãe, Mi—

This is what you wanted, she thought numbly. *This is what you envied.*

Hei gave a sympathetic chirp, nuzzling against her hair. Sohmeng realized she was clenching her fists; her fingers felt stiff as she released them. "Where are the others?" she asked. "I ... there's only four, we're still missing nine."

"Eight," Hei corrected, wry and a little bitter. "We already know Maio Chisong's dead." Sohmeng cursed, shaking her head. Perhaps it was callous, but she—along with the rest of the hmun—had spent so many years assuming the batengmun were dead that she had not expected the confirmation to upend her this way. Somewhere along the line she had convinced herself that if she found the bodies, they would look different, either like proper skeletons or else themselves but sleeping. A foolish notion. A childish thought. But Sohmeng supposed, in the most traditional sense of the word, that she was still a child.

"What . . . what *happened*, though?" she asked, the words falling clumsily from her mouth. "They seem . . . peaceful? I don't know Hei, they, they're dead." She was stuttering, stumbling, her mind tripping over itself for answers it did not want.

Beside her, Hei studied the bodies around the fire. "Their bowls are still here. Perhaps they ate something they shouldn't have. By accident, or on purpose . . ." Their voice softened, lined with regret. "I don't think they would make such a grave mistake. But I couldn't say, Sohmeng."

Unable to bear looking at her dead friends any longer, Sohmeng stole a glance at Hei's face, selfishly hoping for some indication that they were just as afraid as she was. But they were steadfast as she'd ever seen them, bolstering her even as she fell apart. Why was she being so ungrateful? There was no way she'd be able to handle this if Hei was panicking, too.

Sohmeng swallowed. She was not used to being the more emotionally vulnerable of the two. And while she figured *sharing feelings* was a skill she'd eventually have to work out, she didn't feel particularly equipped to try right now. With a shaky nod of determination, she spat one last time upon the ground, then sucked in a breath between her teeth.

"Is there anywhere the rest of them would have gone?" She was cautious to ask Hei about this part of their history. Frankly, it felt offensive to be asking them anything past '*are you okay?*', but she also knew they were her best chance of piecing together what had happened on Sodão Dangde.

Luckily, Hei didn't take it personally. "Tansen Se had talked about leading a small party down the mountain to raise the Bridge themselves, from the Third Finger," they replied, grimacing. "If they did that ..."

"Blacktooth," Sohmeng said, covering her face with her hands and taking a long, slow breath. *Par, Go, Hiwei, Fua, Tang, Sol—* "Okay. Okay. We should try to find them, see if they're somewhere else in the mountain."

Hei wore a guilty expression, speaking as though they were sorry for each word that came out. "Sohmeng, it's mostly likely that ..."

"They're all dead," she interrupted, biting her cheek. "I know, I—I know. I just want to look, to be sure." As grim as their prospects were, it felt wrong turning her back on what they had found. It would feel too much like abandoning friends who had already been abandoned once before. Sohmeng didn't put much stock in the idea of honour, but even she couldn't justify walking back down to Eiji with nothing more than a shrug and a turned stomach. It was better to know. And if she ever did make it back to the hmun on Fochão Dangde, she'd at least have something to make up for ... everything else. Closure for Jinho, and the others.

"Okay." Hei took her hand, turning to face the rows of houses. "Let's look."

Home by home, the two of them searched through the rooms, pushing back privacy curtains and peering through doorways, whistling to hear where the echoes bounced loudest. They started slowly, taking their time with the details. But eventually, their feet picked up pace, and they moved with solemn resignation. Silently, hand-in-hand.

The houses were so similar to those on Fochão Dangde that Sohmeng couldn't help but feel like it was some sort of bizarre homecoming. In a way, it was. After all, the mountains were mirrors to each other, complementary halves of everyone's lives in Ateng. She had been gone for so long that she had nearly forgotten the twin world of her childhood.

As they reached the end of a line, her breath caught. There—a small hut with a rounded right side, a soft cut of purple wovenstone stretching through the awning. She could picture the places where her parents' old travelling skins would hang before they made the crossing, the corner where Viunwei would tuck away his toys so she couldn't get into them. The day they left, she had been so preoccupied with bothering him that she had forgotten to take her favourite pair of dice out of her drawer. She had only realized it halfway across the Bridge, and by then it was too late to turn back.

They'll still be there waiting for you, her mother had reassured her. *Next crossing, during your Tengmunji on Fochão Dangde, I'll hang onto them for you. And then you'll get to come back to them as an adult!*

Hei tugged gently on her hand, clicking inquiringly and jarring her out of the memory. She swallowed, lifting her heels just to prove to herself that she was still capable of moving her feet. "My house," she whispered. "The Sodão Dangde house. This is where I lived before the last crossing. It's where I was born."

"Sohmeng Minhal." They said her name with such tender certainty that Sohmeng's shame nearly forgot to rear its head. She squeezed their hand, only able to nod. This would be a lot easier if her body could respond with the same cool detachment Hei was displaying. With doubt lining every step, she passed through the doorway.

Everything was exactly as she had last seen it: bare and clean, if not dusty from the years of disuse. Her family had spent all morning tidying despite the fact that it was her birthday. That was her least favourite part of being born on the first day of First Par—every other year, she had to clean and pack instead of celebrate. Her father had insisted it was a wonderful gift to celebrate her birth with the great crossing, but it had only ever made her feel overshadowed. An afterthought for the hmun.

She went to the drawer beside her old cot and pulled it open. Her set of dice glowed up at her, and though realistically she knew that it was just the wovenstone's way, she couldn't help but imagine it was intentional, warm with familiarity. For the second time in as many days, she felt tears stinging her eyes. Of all the things to worry about, this was the one that had kept her up at night as a child: her toys, left alone in a drawer to gather dust, gone cold from lack of use. With a trembling hand, she picked them up, watching the soft glow through her fingers, thinking back to all the nights she had spent casting them for her family, pretending she knew how to predict their futures.

Mom will become the leader of the hmun. Dad will turn into an armour bug. Viunwei will grow a big mustache. Grandmother Mi will learn to fly.

I'll become such a good dancer that my dancing will move the mountains closer together. I'll walk all of Eiji, just like Mom and Dad. I'll go even further. Everyone will be my friend.

"Hei?" Her voice was so small.

"Mm?"

"Is this my fault?"

"No."

"You didn't even ask what 'this' is," she choked out, trying to be angry, grasping for a familiar emotion to work with. "You don't even know what I'm talking about."

"No," they admitted, leaning their head against hers. "But I still don't think it's your fault."

Sohmeng squeezed the dice until the edges dug into her fingerbones. Her head was pounding as she resisted tears that had already begun, her thoughts writhing against themselves like snakes caught in a trap. Somewhere, logically, she knew that this, that every bad thing, wasn't her doing. She hadn't broken the Sky Bridge, or sent her parents to their deaths, or killed the batengmun. Deep down, the reasonable part of her brain could recognize that none of these terrible things had anything to do with her. And yet the words, the warnings, shone clear in her mind: *Under two dark moons, the gods are sightless, and the child will be overlooked. Cast out this unfortunate soul, for it brings only disorder to the hmun.*

Grandmother Mi had protected her. Sohmeng had not been cast out, or even been recognized as broken. And though she tried and tried to mold herself properly into the shape of Par, of purpose, her life had still fallen apart around her. Against her better judgment, it was hard not to feel responsible, even when someone was offering her a world where she was not at fault. Especially then.

Godless night, she thought, keenly feeling the sting of the curse in a way she hadn't before, *I'm so tired of this.*

Beside her, Hei stood patiently, running a thumb along their sãoni claws, eyes following the lines of the room as they got acquainted with the space. Turning her attention to them, Sohmeng bristled with curiosity verging on disbelief. Hei had been so afraid while climbing Sodão Dangde, rattled and aggravated and outright distraught. But now, in the place that had caused them so much pain, they were responding with an emotional fortitude that Sohmeng never would have anticipated.

"How are you so calm?" she asked, voice wavering. She didn't want it to sound like an accusation. "This place, everything we've found—you should be the one panicking, not me. Weren't you afraid of coming back here?"

Hei nodded, taking her hand, carefully opening her fingers to see the dice. Their touch was so light that it coaxed Sohmeng into relaxing, into opening herself to a gentler world. "I suppose I was afraid of doing it alone. I was afraid of you leaving when you found out the truth of me. But you didn't. It makes it easier." They rolled the dice over in her fingers, thumbing the symbols on each side. Sohmeng wondered if they had ever seen anything like them before. "And ... I've made a life in Eiji. When Ateng was all I had, losing it was like losing everything. But my world is bigger now. This is just one thing. A terrible thing, yes. But just one."

"Just one thing," Sohmeng murmured, leaning against Hei. She took a deep breath, looking around at her old home one last time, and released it. They slipped from the house like ghosts and returned to their puzzle, drifting, wandering, seeking.

Sixteen

THEY SPENT THE BETTER PART of the afternoon searching the houses, finding each one as uninhabited as the
next. With a small pang of guilt, Sohmeng permitted
herself to take a few things that had been left behind
before the last crossing: a thick blanket, a necklace strung
with wovenstone beads, a small but sturdy cooking pot.
Eiji was bountiful, but it could not provide everything
that existed up in Ateng. At first, Hei was hesitant to bring
down any of these reminders of their old life, but they
had a change of heart when Sohmeng suggested stitching
some of the beads into their hood to imitate throat stripes.
Another hour passed before they both were forced to
agree there were no bodies to be found here.

Not yet ready to return to the main hall, Sohmeng
suggested they check the cave systems. It was slow-going,
physically cramped and mentally nerve-wracking; every
time they entered a new space Sohmeng's heart skipped,
simultaneously hoping that they would and would not

find something. Someone. The walls seemed to close in on her chest, dizzying in their pressure. It was incredible to imagine Hei spending most of their life in this lonely warren.

Hei relieved her discomfort not long after, admitting how unlikely it was that they would find anything inside, particularly any organic matter. "After all," they began, "the armour bugs feed on decay. If anyone was there—"

Sohmeng forced herself to stop listening, raising both of her hands with a loud noise to indicate how little she wanted to hear the rest of that statement. "Nope, Hei, nope. Can't do it."

Hei nodded with an apologetic quirk in their brow, turning their attention instead to a patch of massively overgrown mushrooms which they promptly harvested and put into their thigh bag. Sohmeng plucked her own with a strange feeling in her belly; as much as she had missed the taste of Ateng's mushrooms, she couldn't help but feel like she was robbing the dead.

Eventually, there was only one place on Sodão Dangde they had not yet checked: the site of the crossing.

They pushed through the mountain's winding throat, feeling the change on their skin as the environment slowly gave up its cool glow in favour of the all-warming light that poured in from the mouth of the cavern. Though it had only been a matter of hours, Sohmeng was flooded with relief to be back under Chehangma's gaze.

"It's incredible," murmured Hei with a little trill.

"Without the canopy or the clouds, it's so bright. It's . . . almost frightening."

"There's a reason the godseye splits at night." Sohmeng shrugged. "We couldn't bear it otherwise."

Her laughter died in her throat as she saw the Sky Bridge, perfectly intact, still furled on the Third Finger. Impossible for the batengmun to reach, but always within sight. A nasty punchline. She wasn't sure which mountain had it worse: the one that had seen the disaster, witnessing families falling to their deaths in the midst of their pilgrimage, or the one that had seen nothing at all, and been forced to sit and wait, wondering where they had gone wrong.

Hei made a Sãonipa sound Sohmeng didn't recognize. She forced her gaze away from the Bridge and found them at the wall of the cave, examining the remains of the vines that had hung there. They held up a fistful of fibres that had been pulled into very thin strips, twisted into half-finished braids.

"What are those?" Sohmeng asked.

"Before I was exiled, there was talk of building another Bridge," Hei said, their flat tone indicating how viable an option they thought that was. "We started, but it was obvious that a project of that scale would take . . . I don't know, years." They jostled the vines in their hand, shaking their head. "I told you that some of the batengmun had talked about going down the mountain, raising the Bridge from the Third Finger? They'd have wanted harnesses. None of the rope is left here, and more of the vine was hacked down, so . . ."

"So that's probably it, then." Sohmeng felt her shoulders lower, whether in relief or resignation she could not tell. She remembered all the legends Damdão Kelho had told her, with their clear-cut structure, their tidy morals. Right now, sitting on this flourishing mountain, the untended tomb of her childhood companions, she searched for the logic that would give meaning to what they had found. Nothing came.

She returned to the edge of the cavern and sat down. What lay behind her was enough to make her want to scream, but the world in front of her was so wide that it would simply move on from any attempt she made to disturb it. She tugged at her bangs and looked down at the thick blanket of cloud that had descended over the valley. How strange it was that she could so clearly envision what kind of a day it was in Eiji, that if she closed her eyes she could practically feel the steamy mist teasing over her eyelashes, opening her pores. Above, it was cooler, the air just wet enough to open the lungs for singing, but not enough to cough over or make her clothing stick. She wondered when she had developed the ability to differentiate weather systems in layers. Probably around the time she started squawking like a sãoni.

The thought was enough to make her laugh, a small and slightly hysterical sound. She tilted her head skyward, wondering what it felt like higher, and higher still. All she saw were the shifting colours of the oncoming evening, and the Lantern that had gone cold.

Hei settled by her side and offered her a piece of vine

to strip and braid, a bit of futile work to pass the time and ease the hurt. She took it with gratitude, pressing her fingernail in and watching as the vine began to split.

After a few minutes of wordlessly shredding the plant, Sohmeng gathered her thoughts enough to break the silence. "When do you think they put out the Lantern? I mean, I know *when*, but ... how do you think they decided that was it? That they finally needed to give up and show the hmun they were desperate?"

"Most likely after Tansen's group didn't return," Hei replied, tying together thin fibres of vine. "But that's just my best guess. It was a few months after my exile."

"They really held on for a while, didn't they?" Sohmeng shook her head, thinking of the four bodies they had found, left to wait for companions that would never return. She remembered the hmun's leaders debating whether or not they should put out their own Lantern as a signal that the trouble extended to all of Ateng. They ultimately decided it was dangerous to send such a bleak message to the trapped children. Instead, they sent out rescue after rescue, all of which ended up in dire need of rescues of their own.

"I wish," she started, shaking her head in frustration, "I wish we knew what happened. What *actually* happened. I mean, we assume the four in the hall ate something bad, but we don't know if it was on purpose, or how long they were there for, and it just—it makes me *crazy* not knowing. Just being stuck with more questions. There's just ... there isn't going to be any closure, is there?"

"There never is," Hei said, the corners of their eyes creasing in a peculiar smile. "No bodies, and we wonder if they're dead; bodies, and we wonder how they died. A note and we wonder what went unsaid. A survivor and we wonder about the others. Everyone lives and we wonder what they aren't sharing. All that wondering, that puzzling—I don't know any other animals that do it quite like humans."

"Still working on shaking that quality out of yourself then, oh wise one?" Sohmeng snorted. She had seen the way Hei ran themself in circles over the tiniest details. Traumatic morning or not, she wasn't about to let them think they were above the same stupid lesson she was being forced to learn.

Hei rolled their eyes, gearing up for some retaliatory comment, but was cut off by Sohmeng's laughter. By the moons, it was good to argue. To be petty and difficult and only have to worry about hurting someone's feelings. Because yes, she could be rude. She could be inconvenient, and she could do mortifying things that would have her banging her head against the wall years down the line. But she could also recover from it. She could salvage relationships and work on herself and grow. She could recover from everything, except for death. It was a freeing thought.

Grumbling, Hei shuffled down to rest their head in Sohmeng's lap as they continued picking apart their vine. She smiled to herself, abandoning her own handiwork in favour of playing with Hei's hair and watching the clouds move lazy as porridge. Her eye caught on a place where they were darker, more concentrated, and she wondered if it was raining in Eiji. Hei nuzzled against her, letting out a soft sigh, and Sohmeng found herself comfortable enough to say something stupid. "You know, I had this fantasy of you and me raising the Sky Bridge. Even with no one alive to help, I imagined the two of us just working together and making it happen. Like heroes or something."

"Oh?" Hei asked, scrunching their nose.

"I know," Sohmeng said, swatting their shoulder. "It would never work. Not with only two people, and even with the sãoni to help, it's so high up and far apart that it would just ... not happen. But it was something I was considering, before we got up to this place and ..." And saw the bigger picture. "And saw how bad it looks from here." She eyed the Fingers, the shape of Fochão Dangde in the distance, its own Lantern still softly aglow. Her brother was in there, and her grandmother. The rest of the hmun, just as trapped as the batengmun of Sodão Dangde. "They're going to run out of resources, you know. I'm sure you've thought of that by now. The system can't go on supporting itself with humans depleting it, right? That's the whole point of the crossing."

Hei hummed in grudging acknowledgement. Sohmeng knew the hmun was a sore spot for them, and after hearing their story she could understand why. But she also knew they cared about the mountains, and they wouldn't like the idea of humans desperately pillaging them for survival.

"Without the Sky Bridge, they're going to die in there. Not tomorrow, maybe not even next year. But eventually, they'll starve." It chilled her to say the words so matter-of-factly, but there was power to be found in realism. Once she laid out the facts, she had something to work with. "We can't do it from here with two people, and I don't know where the nearest hmun is that we could ask for help. And we can't work on the First Finger because of the sãoni occupying the area. I'm not dragging the family into another fight, not after what happened last time." Hei clicked softly in surprise, glancing up to meet her eyes with gratitude. Sohmeng leaned down and kissed them. "Don't be a dummy. They're my family, too." She looked once more to Fochão Dangde. "Both of them are. Ateng and Eiji."

The sun pushed through the high clouds, opening pockets of brilliant green in the valley below. Sohmeng took a moment to just admire it all: the treetops, fine as moss from this distance; the dissipating mists, curling and luminous; the stubborn raincloud, rolling and opaque, closer than she would have guessed. She squinted at it, trying to make out the shape.

"Do you want to go back?" Hei asked softly.

"To the hmun?" She bit her cheek, mulling it over. It felt like the answer ought to be more complicated than it was. "I don't know. I really don't think so, not forever. I want my family to know I'm alright, and I want to know they're alright. But with you, in Eiji, I'm ... I'm happier, you know? I'm me. And I don't want to give that up."

"Okay," Hei said, sitting up suddenly, their expression tight and nervous. "I'm glad, I just—I don't want you to stay just because that's what I want. I want you to stay, I do, more than anything. But I want you to make that choice for yourself, otherwise it's just me forcing it on you and—"

"Whoa, whoa," Sohmeng interrupted, giving them a playful shake. "Okay, first of all, that's not what's happening. Second of all, when have I *ever* done something for anyone but myself?"

"You...plenty of times! Even now, you're thinking about the hmun—mmph!" Hei squawked as Sohmeng planted both hands over their face.

"Hei," she said calmly, disregarding their shouts of annoyance, "most of my identity has been thrown into the air in the past few days. For the sake of preserving my sanity, I'm going to need to keep working under the assumption that I'm a selfish jerk. So is it possible for you to just lighten up on all that charming sincerity? For five minutes, maybe?"

Hei bit her hand in response, sitting up with a huff, and Sohmeng kissed them again, pleased that she was still capable of making them blush in the midst of their grumpiness. Talking about all of this was destabilizing, and sort of existentially demoralizing, but at the end of the day, a kiss was still easy. Her fingers found their way back into Hei's hair, and she reveled in the way they gasped into her open mouth, hands grasping at her sides. She shifted into their lap, laughing softly because apparently even a surprise gravesite at the top of the world wasn't enough to stop her from—

"Wait," she said, peering over Hei's shoulder. Down below, the mists had cleared enough that she could better see the dark patch that had been building. That wasn't a rainstorm, that was— "Is that a fire?"

"What?" Hei asked, trying to catch their breath.

"In the forest, I think that's—I think I see smoke."

Sohmeng found herself dumped unceremoniously out of Hei's lap and onto the floor. They jumped up, looking over the ledge without so much as an apology. She was about to yell at them, but then she saw their face. That was a face she knew. She had seen it once before, shadowed by fire and spattered in blood.

They snarled, pacing once, twice, and then thrust out a hand to Sohmeng. "We need to go."

"Now?" Sohmeng asked, allowing herself to be pulled up. "What's happening?"

"I've never seen them make it this far south," Hei muttered, shaking their head. After a beat, they tugged her back into the cave. "There's no time to explain—we have to get down the mountain. The family's in danger."

Seventeen

IF THERE WAS ANYTHING scarier than winding up through the tight passages of the cave systems, it was running down them at full speed.

"Hei!" Sohmeng yelled, out of breath as she struggled to keep up with them. "I know that fires are generally pretty urgent but—but also the jungle is pretty *big*, wouldn't you say?"

Hei scoffed, pushing off the walls with bruising force. Sohmeng fully expected to listen to them hiss about it for the next week, but at least their arm wraps protected them from the jagged stones of the caves. She, on the other hand, had to move with a lot more caution, being bare-armed and loaded down with supplies that now included a cooking pot. "Maybe we could try *not* going so quickly we fall and break our necks?"

Hei leapt over one of the ledges, extending their hands impatiently for Sohmeng. "We only have a couple hours until sundown. By then, the colony will start getting groggy—it'll be too easy to catch them unawares."

"Catch them . . . ?" Sohmeng frowned, lowering herself into Hei's arms. "Is there another sãoni family after them? One that breathes fire?"

"Don't be ridiculous," Hei snapped, turning to resume their sprint. "Their bodies don't sustain nearly enough heat to—"

Sohmeng let out a growl of annoyance, a noise made for halting. Hei snarled out their irritation in response, and all at once she recognized the appeal of sãoni inter-action: quicker than explaining her reasoning, harder to misinterpret. Less room for hurt feelings.

"Not sãoni," Hei said. "Humans."

"Humans? What kind of human would be crazy enough to attack *sãoni?*"

Hei said nothing, only glowering at whatever memory was gnawing at them.

By the time they pushed out of the caves, the light had dimmed to a warm glow. It would have been beautiful if not for their apparent time constraint. In the distance, the smoke was still visible, thick and dark and curd-ling. Sohmeng pulled a sãoni claw out of her thigh bag and used it to cut a fistful of vines hanging above the entryway.

"Sohmeng—" Hei called, already moving down the side of the mountain.

"Keep going, I'll catch up!" The vines came free with a snap; she wrapped them around her arm as she ran to follow Hei. Rush or not, there was always time to restock on resources. And if Hei was right about there being humans brave enough to face off against the sãoni, she wanted to have enough supplies to keep them safe from whatever was headed their way. She secured the pot to her wrist as best as she could while in motion. Riding Singing Violet was enough of a challenge with two hands.

Even with this latest terror looming, Sohmeng found herself beyond relieved to be out of Sodão Dangde. The abandoned hmun had revealed a nest of shame that she never realized she had been feeding. Out in the open, the best parts of herself glinted in the light, bright as the ring that had brought her there.

Despite the dull pang in her ankle, she caught up to Hei, who had not lost the anxiety in their bearing. "Alright, so what exactly are we going up against?" she asked, allowing the urgency in her voice to come through. This wasn't a time where she could indulge Hei's tendency to be stingy with their words.

"Nothing, hopefully. Like I said, they've never come this far south. But I've only ever seen fire burn that hot where they go, so—"

"Who's *they*? Hei, I know you're overwhelmed but—"

They interrupted her with a loud yell of frustration as they jumped over a fallen tree. "I've told you about them before—the humans who've been interfering with the migration cycle."

"Wait, from the Great River?" Sohmeng remembered the map Hei had made in the dirt; scribbles and scratches, a circuit disrupted.

"Exactly. They're not like other humans, Sohmeng." Hei's voice was grim. "They don't stick to their own hmun, they spread like a fungus all down Eiji and any sãoni that cross their path get torched in their sleep—" They broke off into another snarl, too agitated to continue.

Sohmeng felt dizzy. If these humans hadn't thrown off the migration route, then Ateng might never have been attacked. The Sky Bridge might still be whole, the batengmun still alive. It opened a complicated pain inside of her—and now Hei was telling her that the sãoni were in danger as well. She clenched her fists.

I'm not going to lose any more family to this, she thought. She took a furious breath in through her teeth, trying to harden her fear into something useful.

"So what do we do?" she asked. "How do we handle these people, if they're as dangerous as you say?"

"We keep Mama and the family awake," Hei said. "If they keep moving, they'll retain enough heat to stay alert through the night. They'll be snappy and miserable, but it's better than the alternative. More importantly, we have to make sure they stay together. No stragglers. The humans are less likely to attack if the whole colony is there; I don't think they have enough fire-sand to take us all down."

From down the last slope, Sohmeng could hear the chirping and clicking of the two sãoni they had left in the cave. The sound made her heart lift, and momentarily she wondered at the direction her life had gone, where the sounds of the jungle's greatest predators were soothing to her. What had once been the stuff of nightmares was now a reassurance, a promise that things were going to be okay.

The only problem was, Green Bites wasn't in a particularly helpful mood.

"Come *on*," Hei hissed, spitting some Sãonipa curse. "We need to *go!*"

Green Bites huffed in annoyance, resting his chin back on Singing Violet's side and closing his eyes. If it weren't for the urgency of the situation, Sohmeng might have laughed aloud at the petulance he was slinging Hei's way. For their part, Hei looked ready to tear their hair out, making a whole symphony of persuasive, furious shrieks. Green Bites turned away, nuzzling into Singing Violet, who was watching the exchange with mild interest.

"Hei," Sohmeng offered with a nervous laugh, "I don't know if he's going to—"

"Well that's too bad because he HAS to!" Hei shouted, yanking on Green Bites' tail and earning a warning squawk from their brother. "You can show off to your girlfriend some other time, but right *now* you need to move your scaly—"

All at once, Green Bites lunged, snapping close enough to Hei's arm that Sohmeng shouted in surprise. It was one thing when two adolescent sãoni got into a spat, biting and clawing and roughhousing their way through their conflicts. But it was another thing entirely when one of those sãoni happened to be human of body. A nip from Green Bites was more like a chomp, and without Mama around to mediate, Sohmeng could see this going very wrong, very quickly.

She moved to step in, but Green Bites leveled her with a snarl that just about sent her to the floor. Hei lunged between them, barking a challenge. They hardly seemed to notice the danger they were in, so adamant they were on establishing their own dominance. Sohmeng groaned, pressing her palms to her eyes.

"Hei," she called, "do we really have time for this right now?"

They responded with a feral growl, locked with Green Bites in a threatening, circling dance.

Sohmeng threw her hands in the hair, dropping down beside Singing Violet. "Absolutely ridiculous," she muttered. "Moronic. Childish nonsense. The family's about to get served as a freshly-broiled side dish and they decide that *now* is the time for a stripe-measuring contest?"

Singing Violet nudged her nose into Sohmeng's side, letting out the gentle trill that Sohmeng had named her for. She gave the sãoni a sympathetic look. "I know. What do we see in them?" She stroked Singing Violet's nose, cringing as Hei made a lunge at Green Bites, only narrowly dodging the snap that followed in response. Waiting for this to end was going to kill her, assuming it didn't kill Hei first.

But maybe she didn't have to wait. The last time the family was in trouble, she could barely walk, and she had still managed to come to their rescue. Why should she sit around now?

Sohmeng pursed her lips, thinking for a moment before offering Singing Violet a cautious squawk that she hoped meant 'go'. Singing Violet blinked slowly at her. Sohmeng tried again, and once more, until the sãoni repeated the sound to her, shifting attentively.

"Yes!" Sohmeng said, amazed that it was working. For all she could communicate in chirps and growls with Hei, she hadn't had much success with the sãoni themselves. She tried the word again, linking it with the word for 'alpha', and when Singing Violet's gaze moved to the mouth of the cave, she took it as a win.

Before she could doubt herself, Sohmeng climbed onto Singing Violet, grasping the sãoni's head spines as she was lifted off the ground. She sucked air into her lungs and put the sounds together, loudly enough that her voice echoed through the cave. Behind her, the threatening snarls stopped quite suddenly—but before she had any chance to gloat, Singing Violet was mimicking the sound enthusiastically and hurling her body straight down the mountainside.

When Sohmeng finally managed to stop screaming, she took great pleasure in the sound of Green Bites and Hei following behind.

When she was young, Sohmeng's parents had told her stories of the Great River: a swath of water up north, so vast that no bank was visible on the other side. How different the people there must be from her. Even in Eiji, where all of the hmun shared the common ancestor of Polhmun Ão, customs and language varied across the network. Who were these invaders, fearless enough to encroach on the lands of the sãoni, careless enough to endanger every last hmun in the valley? Exactly how much danger was everyone in?

They arrived at the foot of the mountain to a chorus of happy chirping. The reunited sãoni rubbed cheeks and sniffed at each other, curious to scent out where their companions had been. Green Bites puffed up at the attention, clearly thinking very highly of himself. Sohmeng slipped off Singing Violet, giving her head a little kiss, and rushed after Hei, who was already running to Mama. Sohmeng had figured they would launch right into explanatory squawking, but instead they paused with their arms around the alpha's neck, taking in all of the nuzzles and presses she had to give. Despite everything there was to be afraid of, she knew one thing for certain: it was good to be home.

The small army of hatchlings seemed to agree, based on the way they bounded over and knocked Sohmeng off her feet, popping whatever bubble of sentimentality had started to expand within her. She groaned, sitting up straight and trying to pull the cooking pot out of reach before one of them got their head caught in it. Another was nosing at her thigh bag, hissing with disgust but continuing to sniff just the same.

"Oh, get over yourself," Sohmeng laughed. "It's not silvertongue, it's a mushroom. And it's not for you."

The hatchling, undeterred, was about to go in for another sniff when its attention turned to the sound

Hei was making at Mama. Sohmeng would know that sound anywhere—it was the first Sãonipa word she'd ever formed her mouth around completely: alarm. All around her the family mimicked it, more inquisitive than upset, as Mama nudged her face into Hei's belly, trying to calm her anxious child. While Sohmeng understood where Hei's panic was coming from, she could also see how confusing it must have been to the sãoni—everything around them was fine. She stood up, shaking off the clingy hatchlings, and went over to Hei, hoping that she could be helpful.

"What are you telling her?" she asked, giving Mama's nose a stroke.

"I'm trying to warn her," Hei replied, exasperated. "But she doesn't see any danger and I don't know if she can smell it from here and there aren't, Sãonipa doesn't *work* like human language does. We'd have to get closer to the danger in order for her to understand it, and that's the *last* thing we want right now. I need to move everyone further *away!*"

"How many humans are you expecting?" She tucked the cooking pot and blanket into the bag on Mama's head spines, trying to remember how big the fire looked from above. Given the scale of the world around her, she wasn't terribly confident she could make an accurate guess.

"Not . . . not many?" Hei admitted, chewing their lip. "But I don't want to risk anything, not when Mama's eggs are so close to hatching. Even if we could win a fight with them, it doesn't mean it would be—"

Suddenly, Mama raised her nose to the air, eyes narrowing to slits as she let out a series of low, rolling clicks. The other sãoni froze, chins lowered to the ground, eyeing their alpha as they awaited an order. Hei sighed audibly in relief, folding in half like they were ready to kiss the ground. Mama began her alarm cry properly, and the colony echoed it, sending shivers up Sohmeng's spine. She grinned at Hei, getting ready to attempt joining in on the freak-out chorus, when Mama's tone suddenly changed—and she was off running, the other sãoni following close behind.

"No!" Hei shouted, snarling out another curse. "No, no, no, that's not—Sohmeng, come here!"

Hei grabbed Sohmeng's arm, yanking her toward Green Bites and Singing Violet. Green Bites took off, apparently deciding that he'd had enough of indulging Hei's weight on his back for the day, but Singing Violet stopped, flattening herself enough for the two of them to hop on. Sohmeng gave her a happy trill, grasping onto her head spines as Hei mounted behind her and uttered a cry for the sãoni to go.

"Alright," Sohmeng said, bracing herself as Singing Violet propelled through the jungle, "so why are we going *toward* the danger?"

"Because," Hei replied through gritted teeth, "today is apparently the day my entire family reminds me that a shared method of communication does not guarantee agreement."

EIGHTEEN

THE SMELL OF THE SMOKE hit them first, sour and metallic.

The site of the damage was smaller than Sohmeng had anticipated, dry heat shimmering in sheets over plants that had smouldered to crumbling stumps, chalky with ash. She wrinkled her nose against the almost aggressive crackle in the air. The tops of the trees were all but incinerated, leaving a hole in the canopy like the puncture of Hei's needle through sãoni skin; against the singed remains of surrounding trees, the burnished orange of the evening sky seemed poisonous.

The near-constant noise of Eiji had disappeared, monkeys and insects and frogs gone silent in the face of the destruction. Even the sãoni were quiet. The only sound that came was the soft padding of their many feet, the clink of their claws against rogue stones in the underbrush. Suddenly, Sohmeng could hear the pounding of her heart. She did her best to ignore it.

Hei hopped down from Singing Violet, stalking around the site cautiously. With the extent of the burning, it was hard to tell what had been there before. Sohmeng wanted to ask questions, but she was wary of breaking the jungle's sudden hush. She glanced to Mama, who was investigating one particularly charred tree. She'd take her cues from the alpha. How natural it was, to become a part of the pack.

One of their colony cried out from up ahead, and the family followed the signal. Sohmeng trotted behind Hei, nearly banging into them when they stopped abruptly with a hiss of anger. They had found an adolescent sãoni in the cinders, dead from multiple deep, blackened wounds to the neck and belly.

"That's not . . . ?" Sohmeng asked, her stomach squeezing.

"No," Hei confirmed. "Not one of ours." Their expression was dark all the same.

Sohmeng turned to face the worst of the damage. She could see what Hei had meant about the power of these flames—it was as though all the moisture in the grove had been steamed out before it was set alight. "How does anything burn so—"

A series of loud squawks rang through the rainforest, high and urgent. The hatchlings.

Hei's eyes widened; before Sohmeng could think, they were barrelling through the forest on their own two feet, doing their best to keep up with the line of sãoni that were rushing ahead. Sohmeng cursed, leaping back onto the nearby Singing Violet for the sake of speed.

She squeezed the sãoni's head spines, panic fluttering in her chest as if it were her own children crying out, her own siblings.

She didn't need to panic for long. By the time she made it to the scene, Green Bites was nearly upon the aggressor: a human who shone like a god against the beams of light spearing through the canopy. The animal they were riding resembled nothing Sohmeng had seen before, tall and birdlike with wicked talons and a thin, beaked face.

Sohmeng stumbled off Singing Violet, trying to understand what she was seeing. The human's body was plated in glimmering armour that protected them from the bites of the hatchlings, who they were trying to shake off their legs. One bellow out of Mama scattered the hatchlings away from the front lines. Green Bites let loose a snarl that displayed every last one of his teeth, dropping into a menacing crouch; the human's mount screamed back, an ugly, grating sound.

"W-wait," Sohmeng said, entirely unheard. Wasn't there supposed to be a whole party? This was just one human—

Green Bites lunged, and though the human was quick, the sãoni was quicker. He smashed into the human's mount, knocking off the rider and falling into a mess of claws and feathers and scales. The human rolled away, pulling out a sword and charging at Green Bites—but they were too late. With one bite, the sãoni tore the throat from the bird creature, which gave one last gurgling cry before it went limp.

The human let out a wail of their own, raw and mournful, just as Hei stumbled breathless into the clearing. Sohmeng turned to them, grabbing their arm. "We have to stop this," she said, ignoring their baffled look. "There's only one of them, they're alone—we can't just watch them die! We could, we could talk to them! Find out what's going on with the route, why they—"

A horrible noise scraped across the clearing as Green Bites attempted to take a bite out of the human's armour. Sohmeng raised her hands to her face, cringing away from what was sure to be the sight of someone being eaten alive—but the metal did not yield. The human held steady with their forearm between the sãoni's jaws.

Sohmeng took the opportunity to try again. "Hei!" she barked. "Listen to me, *listen*, this is wrong, we have to—"

"They're in our territory!" Hei snarled, turning on Sohmeng with battle-dark eyes, terrified and uncompromising. Something panged in her chest, a question she had not thought to ask before: *How many humans had Hei watched get devoured?*

The thought was interrupted by a teeth-rattling clang as Green Bites' foreclaws came down heavy on the human, sending their helmet flying into the rainforest. Sohmeng tore her gaze away from Hei, struggling desperately against her wordless horror. Without their helmet, the human had no chance of survival, no chance at all. It was done. She braced herself for the carnage.

But Green Bites stopped.

The sãoni reeled back, hissing and gnashing his

teeth, snarling with disgust like the hatchlings had with Sohmeng's mushrooms. Beside her, Hei growled softly in confusion.

The human pulled themself up, disoriented and determined. They reached for their fallen blade, their armour bearing the fresh dents of sãoni teeth. Their face was gentle in its anguish; their hair had come loose from its braid. It was striking silver shot through with black, looking every bit as poisonous as the silvertongue plant itself.

And they come with sãoni-repellant, Sohmeng thought. *Fantastic.*

It only took the human a moment to gather themself. They reached into a satchel and tossed a handful of something grainy and blue onto their sword; it sent flames roiling up the blade with a sound like tearing fabric. The serenity on their face was enough to make Sohmeng stumble back—never had she imagined someone who would face death with such unshakeable calm.

But they weren't facing death, not anymore. Green Bites had retreated, still shrieking and hissing but with no intention of attacking this potentially poisonous foe. The human didn't know that, or else didn't care, and advanced on the sãoni anyway. Their body was precise in its movements; their eyes were locked on their target with bone-chilling resolve. Just before they lunged, a blur of spirit and silver, Sohmeng saw them reach up to tap their right earlobe.

Then Hei was in the human's path, hood pulled overhead, screaming out their own menace.

"Hei, NO!"

The warrior hesitated, seemingly unsure of what they were looking at, and Hei took a swipe with their claws. They didn't last long on the offensive—the warrior's sword might as well have been an extension of their arm for how they wielded it. Hei dodged once, twice, ducking away from the arc of the flaming blade. Sohmeng could see the caution on the warrior's face, the measured footsteps as they blew the hair from their eyes—*godless night*, she thought numbly, *they're holding back*. The stranger was effortlessly side-stepping each of Hei's blows even with one eye on Green Bites, who sat snarling from a distance. Sohmeng thought she might be sick. The dead sãoni in the clearing had been this human's work, no doubt about it.

If Hei kept provoking them like this, they would fall just as fast.

Sohmeng ran into the melee, praying that the warrior would hesitate a second time. "Stop!" she cried, raising her hands. "Please, stop, we—"

Hei jumped in front of her, pushing her out of the way with the same protective noise Mama had used to call back the hatchlings. Mama responded with a roar of her own, loud enough to shake the trees, and the warrior spooked, their blade tearing through the side of Hei's arm. All at once the smell of burning flesh seared the air. Hei grunted in pain but pressed on, apparently unwilling to leave their mate unprotected even as she yelled for them to stop.

Sohmeng's voice didn't go entirely unnoticed—the warrior's gaze caught hers, snagged it like a thorn. For a breathless moment, time warped as they stared at each other and found a lack of enmity, a shared will to survive. *We're both just trying to stay alive here*, she realized.

As if they'd heard her, the warrior sheathed their blade. They raised their fists instead—it only took two blows to bring Hei down. Mama crawled forward, another roar rising from her belly, but Hei lifted themself again, blood pooling at their lip. Sohmeng grabbed them, pulling them back against her and holding on as tightly as she could.

"Stop it," she hissed, her eyes locked on the warrior's. "Hei, stop. *Stop*. They don't want to kill you. Look at them, they're not trying to hurt you—"

"They went for my *brother*," Hei snarled, struggling weakly against her. "They went after *you*, after my family—"

The warrior stepped back, hand on the hilt of their sword, watching the two of them warily before turning to the sãoni. Hesitantly, they stepped forward, narrowing their eyes. Though the colony went wild with furious sound, none dared approach the poison human. The warrior tested their attackers a second time, then a third. When nothing came, they abandoned their stance altogether. They ran to their mount, a pile of feathers and sinew upon the ground, calling something that might have been a name in a voice that sounded to Sohmeng like song. An enemy incarnate. A warrior alone. Haunted, hunted, far from home.

Nineteen

"**LET ME GO,** Sohmeng—!"

Hei was writhing in Sohmeng's arms, their fear overriding all of their better instincts. She pressed her cheek to theirs, looking down at their injured arm with a sympathetic cringe. The blade had cauterized the wound on contact, scorching hot as it was from the blue powder—fire-sand?—so at least there was no bleeding.

Amazingly, the warrior had actually turned their back to the colony. Was it in arrogance, or defeat? Either way, the sāoni did not dare to move closer, and the human made no move to attack, instead kneeling beside their fallen beast with a soft, hurt sound. They were hunched over in grief as they stroked their mount's beak; from where Sohmeng was sitting, it sounded as though they were weeping. It was hard to believe this was the same human who had unflinchingly held their arm between sāoni jaws, who had sent Hei to the ground with such brutal efficiency.

"If they wanted to kill us, I think they would have done it already," she said quietly. She ran through the little she had to work with: dangerous as this human was, they seemed not to want to fight. Plus, they were cornered by an entire colony of sãoni; all the fancy fire displays in the world wouldn't get them out of that alive, even with their hair deterring said sãoni from attacking. "I think we have the upper hand here, Hei."

"I don't trust them," Hei said, out of breath as they gave up on struggling. When she felt confident that they wouldn't lunge biting and shrieking at the stranger the second they were given the chance, she released them.

"Neither do I," Sohmeng agreed. "You've warned me that groups of them are dangerous, and I believe you. I've ... I've never seen fighting like that. But this is just one of them. And that's a good opportunity for us."

"They attacked us! And that other sãoni, you know they killed him, you saw the marks."

"Hei, I have to be honest here," Sohmeng began cautiously. "Can you really *blame* them?"

Hei growled in disbelief, gesturing violently at the human. "You're siding with—"

"Shut up," Sohmeng said firmly, planting a kiss on their head. "I agree with you, Hei. I love the family. I know sãoni aren't mindless killers." Though she did see the irony in her words as the sãoni's threatening noises increased in volume. "But I only know that because they spared my life, and Green Bites certainly wasn't about to do that just now. Neither were you." She broke eye contact, unprepared to grapple with this dilemma after everything else they had worked through today.

Hei ran their hands through their hair with another loud noise of frustration, scowling when the motion tugged at their arm. They went to touch the injury and Sohmeng abruptly swatted their hand away.

"Don't," she said, prompting a grumble from them. For once in her life, Sohmeng took the sulking as a victory. Better that than outright violence. "You know as well as I do that we have to get that cleaned before you start poking at it. But first, I'm going to go talk to them."

Hei let out the Sãonipa alarm, scrambling up after Sohmeng as she stood and brushed herself off. "It's not safe to go alone—"

"Then come with me." Sohmeng shrugged, keeping her eyes on the warrior. "But you have to be nice, which means don't try to murder them. I've had enough death for one day, you know?" The words came out with more bitterness than she intended. "They've probably never seen humans living with sãoni, so let's just do our best to act normal and not scare them off."

Hei clicked in response, confirming to Sohmeng that *normal* had never even been an option. Better to admit that one head-on. She took a deep breath, nodding as though it could clear her head, and cautiously approached the warrior with Hei trailing close behind. All around her, the sãoni raised their voices in protest.

Sohmeng was still several paces back when the warrior turned. Their dark eyes were red-rimmed from crying, their chest rising and falling heavily beneath their shining armour. Though she knew it wasn't actually poisonous, she couldn't help but stare at their hair, the way the silver caught in the sunlight, bright against the black.

The land across the Great River made an entirely different style of human, even beyond the hair. Where Hei was stocky and she was perfectly pear-shaped, the warrior was lean, and taller even than Viunwei. Where her and Hei's skin was the pale amber typical of Ateng, the warrior's narrow face was remarkably sun-bronzed. It made Sohmeng's heart skip to imagine someone who spent so much time directly beneath the godseye. Did their entire hmun live that way? It would explain their power to make the world burn so hot.

She shook herself, swallowing the dryness in her throat and trying to muster up some authority. "Who are you?"

At first the warrior said nothing, their brow furrowing as they stood, their fingers twitching on their sword. Mama let out a low, suspicious rumble, her tail whapping the ground in warning. Sohmeng raised her hands, trying to figure out how to communicate to all parties that no harm was meant. "It's okay. I just want to talk."

"Talk," the warrior echoed, with an expression that might have been hopeful. They tugged at their earlobe nervously, fidgeting with a thick piercing that was partially obscured by their hair.

"Yeah," Sohmeng replied slowly. "Just talk. Who are you? What are you doing this far south?"

She waited as the warrior struggled with what she

had asked. Eventually, they caught on a word. "South," they repeated, reaching into their pocket and pulling out a small damaged box. They opened it, revealing a smashed piece of glass with four ticks in the wood around it. "South, North, East, West."

Beside Sohmeng, Hei made a few unimpressed clicks, crossing their arms over their chest. The warrior looked up at them, gaze lingering on their arm with regret. They opened their mouth to say something, but closed it after a moment, unable to find the words.

"Okay." Sohmeng blew her bangs out of her eyes. "This might be a little more difficult than I thought."

"What, talking?" Hei asked, their voice rife with sarcasm. In any other moment, Sohmeng might have been proud. But now she scowled at them, wishing they would be helpful. Luckily, the stranger caught onto something she didn't.

"Talk, talking ... trade!" they said, their voice raising with excitement as they took a step toward Sohmeng. Hei's shoulders lurched up to their ears; behind them, the sãoni hissed wildly. Reading the crowd, the human stepped back once again, holding their palms out entreatingly. "Talk trade? *Dulpongpa?*"

The realization hit Sohmeng like a ton of sãoni. The cardinal directions, the words for 'talk' and 'trade'—all of this was vocabulary shared between the language of the hmun and the trade tongue, Hmunpa and Dulpongpa. According to legend, all the languages of the hmun descended from Polhmun Ão were relatives, changed only by the passage of time. Every hmun's traders knew Dulpongpa, and many of the words from hmun to hmun were similar enough for travellers to figure out. Her heart lifted as she felt the glow of her parents' last gift to her— she had always wanted to be a trader in Eiji, hadn't she? Time to test her memory.

"*Tswei baheisai khem*," she said. *I know the basics.* She couldn't tell which of the two of them was more relieved. The language sat with a peculiar heaviness on her tongue, awkward from disuse. In general, its sounds were harsher than those of her hmun's language, rough like untumbled stone, but not entirely unwieldy. With a pang in her chest, she sent up a prayer of gratitude for Grandmother Mi's insistence on her practicing, even after the fall of the Sky Bridge. "Enough to get by."

"More than I," they replied, placing a hand to their chest. Rather, *his* chest, as he had used the masculine 'I'. This was one of the benefits of Dulpongpa: gendered personal pronouns to make up for differences in gender systems within the dialects and the individual hmun. Despite Sohmeng's lack of fluency and the distraction of the warrior's musical accent, she was thankful for this particular linguistic feature; she had no idea how she would even begin translating a discussion about phasal gender systems.

"What's your name?" Sohmeng asked, figuring it was best to get to the point.

His answer came out in one long stream, lilting and turning in a way that left Sohmeng completely unable to follow it. He caught the confusion on her face and quickly followed up with, "Ahn. Ahn is alright."

"Ahn," she repeated, hearing the way her own accent added a soft nasality to the consonant. She thought it sounded nicer that way, and he didn't bother to correct her. She cleared her throat, allowing herself to step closer to him despite Hei's soft growl of protest. "I'm Sohmeng—" Her voice caught. Sohmeng what? Par? Minhal? She could feel the seconds passing. Now was not the time for her to grapple with how she was going to begin self-identifying. She grimaced out a smile. The feminine 'I' was enough for now—it got the point across. "Sohmeng is alright."

The warrior, Ahn, tilted his chin in acknowledgment, tapping his unpierced left ear. Was that how they greeted people across the Great River? Before she could ask, Ahn's gaze had landed on Hei, who scowled and averted their eyes. "And your companion . . . ?"

"Hei," Sohmeng said, ignoring the annoyed huff that came from beside her. She wasn't sure if Hei could even follow the trade tongue, but she figured they would interrupt if they found anything truly objectionable. They'd certainly been more difficult for less. "You'll have to forgive them, they're not much in a talking mood. Which makes sense, seeing as you just attacked our hmun."

Ahn frowned uncertainly. That was to be expected; like Sohmeng had said to Hei before, two dirty humans and a horde of screeching sãoni weren't exactly a conventional family. As far as she knew, no hmun in history had ever cohabitated with sãoni, certainly not as societal equals. She crossed her arms, waiting as he measured out his words.

"...in the North?" he asked cautiously, his shoulders squared as if preparing for conflict.

"The North?" Now it was Sohmeng's turn to be confused. "No, right here. This—this is our hmun!" She gestured to the sãoni, who kept right on with their snapping and snarling, illustrating what a completely sane duo she and Hei were to willingly ride along with them.

Ahn's eyebrows raised and he opened his mouth slightly before closing it. "Ah." A painfully long beat of silence passed between them, and then: "I am sorry, but I do not think I understanding—"

Hei, apparently deciding they'd heard enough, threw their hands into the air with a loud, aggravated hiss. Faster than Sohmeng could follow, Ahn's hand was back to his sword, his footing set like he had made a deal with the earth to keep him standing. As though they'd just been waiting for an excuse, Hei's fingers sank back into their sãoni claws, a snarl tearing from their lips as Green Bites roared behind them.

"Okay, alright, enough—" Sohmeng stood between them, one hand placed on Hei's chest, the other hovering above Ahn's. She gave Hei a sharp chirp that settled them down into some quiet clicking, then turned to face Ahn. "No swords! Seriously. Everyone is tense right now, and you going all ... god-bodied sun warrior isn't really doing anything to help. The situation, I mean." She laughed a little too loudly, giving his armour a pat with an unceremonious clank. "I'm sure it's doing something for someone."

Mercifully, he didn't seem to hear her, or understand. Instead, he took her hand with a perplexed look, curiously tapping the ring on her finger. The ring that was molded in the same star-bright silver as his armour.

If that wasn't some kind of sign, she wasn't sure what was.

"Sohmeng I do not like this man," Hei muttered, placing their hand over hers.

"I know," Sohmeng said, her mind still racing as she sought out the best way forward. "Thank you for being so patient with me."

Hesitantly, Hei slipped off their claws in order to examine their arm, wrinkling their nose in distaste. Sohmeng turned back to Ahn. "These sãoni, and Hei and I, we are family. Hmun. Down here. Eiji. Do you understand?" She watched him take in Hei, their sãoni skin clothing, the dark circles around their eyes. With far more kindness than Sohmeng had first offered Hei, he nodded. "You killed one of the sãoni. Not ours. But a sãoni."

"Sãoni?" he repeated, gesturing to the creatures that were watching the spectacle.

"Sãoni." Sohmeng nodded. "They're good. Well, no, some of them eat humans. But not all of them, not ours, and it's—complicated. Listen, I don't want to hurt you, or leave you down here to be found by some other sãoni that *do* eat people, but I can't help you unless I know you won't hurt my family." For Hei's sake, she repeated herself in Hmunpa, watching Ahn think on it all the while. Once more, the cool facade on his face cracked, and he pointed to the fallen creature behind him.

"Lilin," he said firmly, the hurt in his voice ringing clear through the jungle. "My family."

"I'm sorry," she said, immediately knowing the words to be inadequate. She lowered her eyes to the ground, cringing at the maimed body of the creature. Lilin. It was harder when things had names.

Beside her, Hei was watching them intently. Even without the language, the subject of the conversation was clear, the emotional response thickening the air like heavy morning mist. Without any warning, they turned away from Ahn and Sohmeng, walking up to Green Bites and giving him a firm whack on the nose. He snarled in response, snapping at Hei, who whacked him again, provoking the already-riled sãoni into further aggression.

Sohmeng sucked in a breath, testing her trust in the family as she kept herself from yelling for Hei to stop. Hei wouldn't do anything to get themself killed, she told herself, and their idiocy on the way down the mountain pointed to a larger pattern of how they and Green Bites tended to roughhouse. Of course, that didn't make it any less jarring when the sãoni clamped his jaws around Hei's arm.

Ahn reacted before Sohmeng could, reaching for his sword as they cried out in pain. But Green Bites let go, clicking and growling, licking at the small puncture wounds that circled Hei's bicep just below where Ahn's sword had cut through. They looked to Ahn silently, their face tight with pain. He seemed to understand; he took out his sword, placing it on the ground in front of him. With that sorted, Hei walked over to Mama and stuck their arm into her cheek, letting her saliva do its work.

Sohmeng rubbed her temples, considering the value of using one's words rather than dramatic gestures to make a point. "Glad that's dealt with," she said dryly. She turned to Ahn. "Are there others with you? Or are you alone?"

"I am alone," said Ahn with a little nod. "Others are . . . North? Far. Lose."

"Lose? Lose what?"

"I lose—the others."

She thought of the wooden box he had presented, the repetition of the cardinal directions. He had gotten separated from his hmun, just the same as she had. While she knew he was dangerous, or at the very least came from a dangerous hmun, she could not help the stab of empathy that went through her.

"Hei?" she called, switching back to Hmunpa. "It's just him down here. He says the rest of them are up—"

"North," Hei interrupted, pulling their arm from Mama's mouth with a scowl. "Far north. Most likely the northernmost part of the sãoni migration path." They nodded, pressing a hand gently to Mama's nose. "Ask him how many there are in his hmun."

"Once the family gets back on their route, we could bring him—"

"Ask him." Hei's voice was uncompromising, their eyes harsh but not unkind. The intensity made Sohmeng falter. She did her best to keep her voice casual as she posed the question.

"Few hundred," Ahn said easily. Sohmeng opened her mouth, about to protest the possibility of a number that great, when he continued his estimate. "Next year, ten hundreds—no, sorry, one thousand. More, maybe."

Sohmeng turned to Hei, a shiver going up her spine. The shadow hanging over them told her that she did not need to translate these numbers. It was probably for the best; she felt woozy just at the idea of speaking them. The disruption in the jungle wasn't a matter of one small hmun stepping out of line—it was an all-out swarm. Like the sãoni climbing Fochão Dangde, swiping down whatever stray humans they found, disregarding what it meant for the world that was trying to thrive there. A disruption in the system.

And now, standing before them was one small part of that disruption, laying down his sword and giving them his name.

Sohmeng Minhal had never been one to hesitate once she'd made a decision, so when she approached Ahn, it almost felt as though someone else was in her body, maneuvering her limbs and steering her destiny. She got up on her tiptoes and grabbed the man by his shining chest plate, rubbing her cheeks against his with no inhibition. He let out a surprised noise, trying to extricate himself from her grip as she nuzzled into his hair, making

a show of how little poison it contained. Around her, the
sãoni rumbled among themselves, trying to make sense
of how one of their own was acting out.

"Sohmeng," Hei said cautiously.

"His hmun is what got all of this trouble started, right?
If we want to know what's coming, if we want to *fix* it,
we're going to need his help." She pulled back with a nod
of certainty, appraising the newest member of their colony.
For the most part, he was staring back at her in stunned
silence. She gave his shoulder a firm pat. "Welcome to the
family, Ahn."

"I—family?" Ahn asked, looking from her to Hei to the
sãoni. A hatchling wiggled away from under Mama's mid
legs, coming over to investigate Sohmeng's new friend.

"Hey," she said with a shrug, "just be thankful I didn't
bite you."

Hei crept up beside Sohmeng, taking her hand with a
familiar frown. Wary, tender. The face of the mate she had
decided to share a life with. Sohmeng ran her fingers over
their sãoni claws, offering Hei the most reassuring sound
she could: a chirp and three clicks. A name. A promise
that she knew exactly who it was that she was choosing
to stand by.

That was what it meant to live in Eiji. No matter how
strange the family or sightless the gods, Sohmeng could
exist here precisely as she was: all of her loudest, wild-
est parts in balance with her greatest vulnerabilities. If
Tengmunji was about discovering one's purpose, then
Eiji held more room for her growth than any mountain

ever could. If Sohmeng had truly been born outside the realm of the gods, she owed nothing to their laws. The only person she had to answer to was herself.

"Let's get you both cleaned up," she said, smiling in spite of everything. "We have a lot to talk about."

And so Sohmeng Minhal took the first step into her adulthood without permission, without any shame to be found.

THE SÃONI CYCLE

WILL CONTINUE IN 2020

ACKNOWLEDGEMENTS

This book was born out of two things: fighting writer's block, and finally accepting that I had no choice but to write about what I love. As it turns out, I mostly love astrology, queerness, and giant lizards. Was anyone surprised? Not really.

I don't know if I can ever fully express how grateful I am to everyone who supported me through this journey, but I can start by listing some names:

First, my hmun—my Grandma Ronnie instilled a passion for speculative fiction that has made me the person I am today. The Silver in my name is hers. My Mom read the first draft of "Two Dark Moons" with the critical eye of a teacher and all the pride of a Jewish mother. My father showed me Jurassic Park when I was far too young to watch it, launching me into a love of dinosaurs. I also have to thank my brother Ryan for studying medicine— not only did he take the pressure off me as the artist of the family, but he also helped me figure out how not to kill Sohmeng when I threw her off a mountain.

Where my brother taught me how to keep Sohmeng alive, Sophie Delville spared me the grisly research involved with the dead. Jen Frankel showed me more love than I knew what to do with, and drank the character tea blends I made for Sohmeng when the book was in its infancy (hibiscus, lime, nilgiri black tea). Cortni "Supportni" Fernandez dutifully attended every round of Art Prison, and got hostile enough when I mentioned cutting things that I began to have faith in my writing. Courtenay Barton got me back into a love of reading via YA after years of that joy being stolen by depression. Katie Fontes helped me love astrology so much that I made up my own system. Elisa Murphy sat poolside with me while I cried about being too loud as a child.

Haley Rose gave me the cover of my dreams, and indulged all of my shouts of "It's a real book!!" The International House of Goblins has uplifted me time and time again: Urs' puns were the foundation for Hei's name, and Irene Zhong encouraged me through shouts of *AVI* with all the horror of Viunwei Soon. Carisa Van de Wetering sent me the memes that got me through. Spenser Chicoine talked me off the ledge and reviewed everything I missed in biology class. Brianna Tosswill's drawing of me moping in a blanket helped pull me out of editing hysteria.

A special, breathless thank you to Natalie Lythe. As always, I must love you or die—I asked for a beta reader and was given an additional editor, counselor, and dear friend. I'm yours to bite, always.

ACKNOWLEDGEMENTS

Thank you to Toronto NaNoWriMo 2018 for helping me finish this beast, to Can*Con 2018's Hopepunk panel for opening me up to tenderness, and to the many supportive voices on social media. Reading JY Yang showed me that I could be as queer on paper as I am in person. Rachel Hartman's *Tess of the Road* was one of the first books I read upon immigrating to Canada, and helped me unpack what needed to be worked on in order for the Sohmeng in me to grow. Musically, I owe a great debt to Aurora, Kishi Bashi, Huun-Huur-Tu, Kevin Penkin's *Made in Abyss* soundtrack, Keiichi Okabe's music of *NieR*, and Xiao Xingni for her harp cover of *Violet Evergarden*'s "Never Coming Back". Pamenar Cafe and Boxcar Social were sacred writing spaces.

A peculiar and particular gratitude to the characters of mine that were not yet willing to cooperate—you opened up the space for Hei and Sohmeng's story to begin. I'll get to you eventually.

Finally, Sienna. Naming systems, lunar nonsense, relentless editing, book design, worldbuilding debates, *Shale*—you make it all possible. This book would not be here without you, and I am honoured to love and be loved by you every day. You found me at the bottom of a mountain and brushed me right off. Thank you.

With love and a bite,
Avi Silver
April 2019
Toronto

Glossary

Ama—the small red moon, feminine; ruler of reason and material matters

Ateng—the hmun's name for their mountain range, literally "Above"

batengmun—initiates; singular would be "tengmun"

chandão—sibling

chapongão—parent

Chehang—the big white moon, masculine; ruler of emotion and spiritual matters

Chehangma—the sun, viewed by the hmun Ateng as the combined eyes of the moons Ama and Chehang

dangde—mountain

damwei—the third party required to make a baby, either a surrogate or sperm donor; affectionately referred to as "damdão"

Dulpongpa—the trade language of the valley's hmun network

Eiji—the valley below Ateng, home to a network of hmun

fochão—brother

Fochão Dangde—the mountain the hmun is currently trapped in; "Brother Mountain"

hãokar—the exiled; literally "without family"

hmun—a village/community

Hmunpa—the language of the hmun; Sohmeng uses this term for Atengpa because it is the language of the hmun she lives in

pashasão—mother

Polhmun Ão—an ancient civilization that was destroyed in a planet-shaking catastrophic event; occasionally referred to as "The Last City"

sãoni—great big lizards that occasionally eat humans; friends?

Sãonipa—the click-and-growl language of the sãoni, as named by Sohmeng

sodão—sister

Sodão Dangde—the mountain the batengmun are trapped in; "Sister Mountain"

tanghilão—father

Tengmunji—Ateng's initiation into adulthood

tengmun kar—uninitiated; not actually an insult, but Sohmeng is feeling sensitive

PATREON | THE SHALE PROJECT

A massive thank you to everybody who supports us on Patreon!
You make this work possible; we love you to the moons and back.

Carisa Catherine

Spenser Chicoine

Emily Colgan

Lily Ray Davis

Rebecca Diem

Laurence Dion

Dana Doucette

Cheryl Hamilton

KTFartes

Minh

Natalie Lythe

Cass Meehan

Susan Meehan

Joy Silvey

WWW.PATREON.COM/WELCOMETOSHALE

About the Author

Avi Silver is a queer, nonbinary author based in Toronto. Their previous work on Shale includes the web serial "Tales from a Library". When they aren't writing, you can find them playing their baby harp, destroying the gender binary with all due flair, and perfecting their chocolate chip cookie recipe. *Two Dark Moons* is their first novel. You can find them on Twitter @thescreambean.

About the Project

The Shale Project is a multimedia storytelling initiative roughly in the shape of a planet. It's about three things: top-notch worldbuilding, daring and exploratory fiction, and the philosophy that art is medicine. You can discover what else it has to offer at www.welcometoshale.com

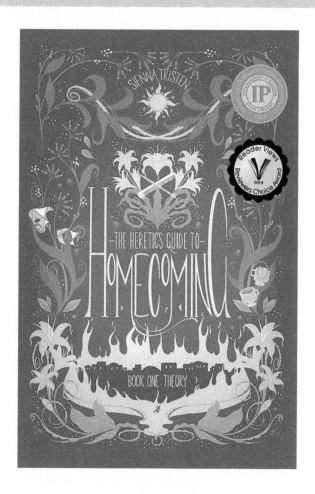

The Heretic's Guide to Homecoming
Book One: Theory

Sienna Tristen

"Compelling and complicated in all the right ways. . . . beautifully written, not just in mythos but also in its treatments of its characters. Tristen writes on these emotions in a way that is rich with understanding and empathy."
-Reader Views